LINDSAY'S ESCAPE

Lindsay's escape was Hillcroft, a run-down riding school. She needed to escape, from her cousin Martin, who considered their future marriage a foregone conclusion, and from her over-possessive father . . . Her first visit to the riding school led to an unfortunate encounter with an irate farmer, but Lindsay was not going to allow anything to turn her from her plan. She bought the riding school, but problems piled up and she seemed to have inherited the run of bad luck suffered by her predecessor.

ANNE NEVILLE

LINDSAY'S ESCAPE

Complete and Unabridged

LINFORD
Leicester

First published in Great Britain in 1982 by
Robert Hale Limited
London

First Linford Edition
published 2006
by arrangement with
Robert Hale Limited
London

British Library CIP Data

Neville, Anne
    Lindsay's escape.—Large print ed.—
Linford romance library
1. Love stories
2. Large type books
I. Title
823.9'14 [F]

ISBN 1–84617–184–9

Published by
F. A. Thorpe (Publishing)
Anstey, Leicestershire

Set by Words & Graphics Ltd.
Anstey, Leicestershire
Printed and bound in Great Britain by
T. J. International Ltd., Padstow, Cornwall

This book is printed on acid-free paper

For
Gerry Dunn and Sue Curtis
at the Grovely Riding School
and also for Annie

1

By the time I had driven half a mile down the narrow, muddy track, I had begun heartily to wish I was driving something bigger and higher off the ground than my low slung white Italian sports car. It had brought me effortlessly and speedily all the way to Wiltshire from Lancashire but it evidently baulked at country lanes ankle deep in mud and deeply entrenched by tractor treads. The lane was bordered on both sides by good old fashioned hedgerows, hawthorn, blackthorn and high, steep banks covered by remnants of last autumn's Old Man's Beard. I was so low down in the sports car that I felt hemmed in on all sides and very ill-equipped to meet any on-coming vehicle.

That I encountered only one such vehicle would have been counted as fortunate but for the fact that this particular vehicle happened to be a very large tractor pulling an open topped trailer loaded with bales of hay. The thing loomed round a corner towards me and both I and the tractor driver rammed on our brakes just feet away from disaster — at least, it would have been a disaster for *me* though I doubted that a collision would have meant much more that a dent to the tractor. My heart was hammering anxiously. I knew that it was I who should do the backing up but quite honestly, driving forward had been bad enough and I felt utterly incapable of reversing down that lane. There was a long moment of stalemate while I stared at the indistinct face of the tractor driver through the muddy windscreen. Slowly I wound down the nearside window and waited. The driver seemed in no hurry. I watched him light a cigarette and blow a cloud of smoke into the cold air. Then, in a maddeningly casual way that I arrogantly supposed was typically rural, he called:

'Well, are we going to stay here all day, or are you going to back up?'

The tone was insolent to the extreme and immediately brought out the very worst in me. My excuse is that my nerves were all to pieces because of the drive and I didn't fancy making a fool of myself in front of a stranger. The real truth, of course, was that I had been raised to the certain knowledge that no one talks to Lindsay Henderson in that tone of voice, especially not someone driving a tractor! A reprehensible attitude to be armed with when deciding to live in the country, but there it was. I sat back in my comfortable leather seat and switched off the engine.

After another couple of minutes, during which I turned on the radio and pretended keen interest in the burblings of the Radio Two disc jockey, the tractor driver finished his cigarette, flicked the stub into a nearby puddle and jumped down from the cab actually into the puddle. Since he was wearing very ancient looking denims tucked into rubber boots, this obviously did not matter. He walked across to the car, his movements every bit as arrogant as my own, leaned into the car and switched off the radio.

'Lady, apart from a little thing like sheer good manners, which you obviously don't possess, it must be fairly obvious even to a moron that if anyone has to do the reversing it should be you. There's a passing point about fifty yards back. So get going. I've got a herd of hungry Guernseys waiting.'

I was unnerved to say the least. For one thing, he didn't speak with a good old Wiltshire accent as I had expected from the tractor and the clothes but with a beautifully cultured voice that would not have been out of place at one of Daddy's cocktail parties. Also, at close quarters he looked a good deal less harmless than I had at first thought, and totally unlikely to be intimidated — in other words, big and broad and tough, with a look in his cold blue eyes to match.

'Why should I?' I bluffed, my voice not nearly as confident as I would have wished. 'I have as much right on this lane as you have.'

'That's a matter of opinion. And as to 'why' — perhaps you'll understand this. Because if you don't I shall just keep on going and this little heap of foreign rubbish won't last two minutes against a good solid Leyland tractor.' His eyes glinted as he said this so that, though I gasped: 'You wouldn't dare!' I was a good deal less certain of this than I sounded.

'Don't you be too sure of that,' he muttered, and suddenly wrenched open the car door. 'Get out! If you won't reverse, I'll damn well do it for you.'

I had a fleeting vision of what my father would say if he were able to hear this conversation and was almost amused by the thought. Putting as much haughtiness into my expression as I could in the circumstances, I let my eyes drop to his feet in the Wellington boots. He was standing in a particularly muddy spot and the boots were covered with mud, bits of straw and I dreaded to think what else.

'I have no intention of letting you get into this car in those!' I said stiffly and switched on the engine. He grinned sourly and slammed the door shut before returning to the tractor. He did not, however, climb back into the cab but stood by it, hands thrust deep into the pockets of the navy blue duffel coat he wore, and watched me. Feeling ridiculously nervous because of this steady scrutiny — the brute was obviously one of those males who consider all women inferior and women drivers particularly so — I reversed the car fairly successfully half the distance to the lay by. Here the lane turned in a fairly sharp curve and the surface at that point was even more pitted and slippery than anywhere else; it was with a sickening sense of inevitability that I felt the rear wheels sliding away from my control. I swung the wheel furiously but the back of the car swerved sideways and slid gently into a ditch. I rammed my foot on the accelerator but all I got for my pains was a horrible sickly sound as the wheels bit harmlessly into the mud.

My protagonist walked over and, standing hands on hips, looked in silence at the rear end of the sports car. He said nothing to me at all but returned to the tractor, took down a tow rope and proceeded to attach it to the front bumper of the car, and the other end to the tractor. It was all done with the swift efficiency of someone accustomed to doing such things and in less than ten minutes the sports car was standing firmly on its four wheels again. By then I was shaking with submerged rage, humiliation and just plain, good old-fashioned fury. So angry was I that as I sat watching the man unhitch the tow rope, my hand itched on the steering wheel and my foot yearned to ram down on the accelerator and run him down. Actually I was shaking so badly that I could not have driven the car.

Again he came and wrenched the door open. 'Get out!' he said.

'I won't. I told you, I'm not having . . . '

'Damn you, woman. Get out of this bloody car before I drag you out. I don't know what the hell you're doing driving along here in this ridiculous heap of tin anyway, and I don't much care, but some people have got work to do and I've already wasted far more time than necessary here. So get out!'

I got out. It was bitingly cold and though I wore a calf length woollen skirt and leather boots, my jersey was thin and my sheepskin coat was in the car. I stood on the only dry bit of ground I could find, a miserable tuft of grass, and watched my expensive Italian sports car being driven with consummate ease back into the lay by. I prayed for something terrible to happen but of course nothing did. The car was driven smoothly off the lane and the man got out. He walked across to me, striding through the puddles and ruts alike and halted briefly in front of me.

'Next time you decide to rough it, keep right away from me. Townies like you ought to have to serve notice that they're going to disrupt the country-side.'

'I am *not* a townie!' I protested indignantly, finding my voice at last. 'Of all the high handed, arrogant men I've ever come across . . . '

'If you want to swap insults, lady, you'd soon find yourself outdone. But I've wasted enough time as it is without doing more than to tell you that you're a spoiled, ill-mannered brat who prob-ably deserves a bloody good spanking!'

By then, as I watched the tractor and trailer finally chug on past, the driver looking as cool and aloof as if nothing had happened, I had half a mind to give up and go home. If it wasn't for the fact that that would entail making a one hundred and eighty degree turn in the lane, *and* possibly meeting up with *him* again, I might well have done so. Which, as it turned out, would have been a great pity.

I went over to the car, put on my sheepskin coat and spent a few unprofitable minutes trying to get some of the mud off the highly impractical but — until then — beautiful white rug that was now more of a black rug. I swore low and furiously and hated the male sex with all the bitterness of a true feminist, which I was not. I have always believed a woman's greatest strength lies in her femininity and was not about to abandon mine. I knew I was beautiful for I had been told it enough times throughout my life and it has always been an easy way out to use that to get my own way. For the first time in all my twenty-four years I had met someone *not* affected by my honey blond hair or green eyes and it was galling to the extreme. The fact that deep down I knew I had been totally and unforgiveably in the wrong did nothing to ease my sense of outrage at having been hard done by.

I drove on, encountering nothing else that moved, and eventually came to where another track met the lane, a track that led to a somewhat broken down gate with an equally knocked about wooden notice tacked to it. The notice, readable only at close quarters, said HILLCROFT RIDING SCHOOL and in smaller letters: *daily hacks — full and grass liveries accepted*. I switched off the engine and sat still a moment, looking at the battered notice, then got out of the car and crossed the lane, leaping over a large puddle. I rested one hand on the gate post and looked in. After a few minutes the tension in me drained away. The encounter with the Male Chauvinist Pig retreated into unimportance and I knew I was glad I had come.

It was exactly what I wanted, just what I had been looking for. I felt at home just standing there and, in a way, I thought fancifully, that's just what it was, a homecoming. The sense of *déjà-vu* hit me with unexpected force, one of those strange 'I've been here before' moments that some people experience often and others never.

It was very quiet as I stood there on that chill March afternoon, with the row of beech trees in the distance shrouded with mist and the sky a lowering grey. The only signs of life were of an animal nature, a tortoiseshell cat groomed herself in a leisurely fashion on one of the few dry patches in the yard, two sparrows pecked about in the mud, a grey pony looked curiously at me over the bottom half of its stable door. I looked round slowly, contemplating the big step I intended to take, missing nothing there was to be seen. I felt a little tremor of excitement that was almost a sensation of sickness — there was a trace of fear in it too. I had never been a rebel, never felt the need, even as a teenager, and this was so much more than a normal kicking over of the traces.

The yard was built on traditional lines with the buildings round three sides of a quadrangle, the fourth side being this hedge and wall in which was set the gate I was standing by. There were perhaps twenty loose boxes that I could see and a high building that was presumably an office and/or tack room. At one corner a gate stood open, apparently leading into an open area beyond. The yard was very uneven, very muddy and filled with large puddles; there was a mounting block consisting of a huge lump of untreated stone, and a water trough. A closer scrutiny revealed signs of decay, flaking green paint on the doors, a piece of guttering hanging dangerously above one stable; the very gate by which I stood was unsafe, with the hinges loose, the wood rotten and splintering as I touched it.

I must have been there some ten minutes when the peace of the afternoon was disturbed by the sound of approaching hoof beats and round the corner of the lane, in the opposite direction from which I had come, appeared a string of about ten horses and ponies that reached me and turned into the yard. I moved across to the car and leaned on the bonnet, watching as they passed, conscious of more than one pair of curious eyes turned in my direction. The string was led by a middle-aged woman on an ugly looking dun gelding and the rest of the riders were girls, all under fifteen with the exception of the one at the rear, a girl slightly older, very slender and pale but riding the chestnut cob with excellent skill. The woman in the lead shot me such a penetrating look that I felt there was little about me she had missed, but the pale girl gave me a shy smile that I found easy to return.

In the yard the riders dismounted and I now saw more signs of human activity as four or five girls of varying ages erupted from the vacant loose boxes or from the tack room; saddles were removed, bridles replaced by halters and the animals led off to their stalls. I looked critically at the ponies; they were sturdy and well cared for, with nothing special about their breeding apart from the good looking chestnut the pale girl had been riding. I wondered briefly about my own mare, Lady. She would look out of place here yet I knew I could not give her up, not as I intended giving up the Italian sports car that Daddy had given me for my twenty-first birthday, and that the beast of a tractor driver had termed that 'little heap of foreign rubbish'. I would exchange that for something sensible, a Land Rover perhaps; something useful that could pull horse boxes if necessary. But Lady was different. I had owned her eight years, since she was an unschooled two-year-old. Together we had been to many shows, won a few rosettes, shared many happy rides. No, Lady had to come with me. It was the most complicated part of The Plan, but not impossible.

The Plan. In my mind the words had been given capital letters from conception, and I smiled at the thought. The smile was unexpectedly echoed by the middle-aged woman in the yard who seemed to think it had been aimed at her. She walked towards me.

'Miss Henderson, it would be?'

'Yes.'

'I'm Julia Symonds. Nice to see you. Sorry I wasn't here to greet you. We were a bit late starting today. We've finished now until the two o'clock ride so come and have a look round.'

She was older than I had at first thought, nearer fifty than forty, and much aged by the weather brown skin and tired eyes. The hand that clasped mine firmly was hard and calloused. Her hair was iron grey and untidy, her cord trousers and jumper little less than disreputable. She looked as lacking in care and attention as the yard did, but her smile was warm and friendly and at least the neglect had not spread to the horses.

'You'd better bring your car inside,'

she told me. 'Put it through that gate there, next to my Land Rover. A few of the local farmers use this lane and you don't want that lovely car hit by a tractor.'

In view of my recent experience, I hastened to comply. There was always the possibility that the 'MCP' might come back after delivering the hay to his Guernseys and I had no wish for another confrontation. I drove through the open gate at the far side of the yard and parked beside the Land Rover. I could now see a large field where a few ponies grazed, and an open space that I presumed was the schooling area. It was in a frightful condition, inches deep in mud and totally unusable. I thought of the man-made surfaces now available, that I had seen used in other riding schools, spread on well drained ground and capable of holding out against almost all weathers. Expensive but better than having a school that couldn't be used at all in the winter. I returned to the yard, having taken another quick look at the ponies in the field. Miss Symonds was leaning on a stable door watching the ugly dun she had been riding earlier with great affection.

'This is Captain,' she told me cheerfully. 'He's an ugly brute and bad-tempered, but all my own. He isn't for sale as the others are.'

I wasn't likely to lose much sleep over that, I thought, looking at the dun with critical eyes. I realized I would have to change my ideas a good deal — the horses and ponies I had been accustomed to all my life would not have made good riding school animals. But still, I saw no reason to lower my standards too much.

'Come into the tack room,' Miss Symonds said. 'I'll make us some coffee. I always keep the makings in here.'

'Please don't bother on my account.'

She glanced sharply at me, the look assessing and critical. I knew why, for I, too, had detected the cool, rather aloof tone in my voice. It wasn't entirely my fault. I had been raised to be aloof and distant. We Hendersons 'kept ourselves to ourselves' in the worst possible way. I could almost hear my cousin Martin saying: 'The trouble with you, Lindsay, my sweet, is that you lack the common touch.' Well, that was when I was nineteen and most definitely did not have the common touch. In part, at twenty-four, I still didn't. There was an arrogance in the Hendersons that was as difficult for me to shake off as it had been for me first to acknowledge its existence. I knew it was there. I had recognized it in Daddy, in all my various and numerous cousins, uncles and aunts. I knew it was in myself and heartily and sincerely wished it was not. I thought I had lost it but the incident with the tractor driver, and now Julia Symond's look, told me most clearly that I had not.

'It's for my own sake, my dear,' Miss Symonds now said, plugging in an electric kettle. 'I've been hard at it since six this morning.'

While she made the coffee, I sat on a wooden stool and looked around. We were in a very large room with a high beamed roof and light coming in from two cobwebby skylights. Mainly because of the cobwebs, the far reaches of the room were immersed in gloom. The smell was predominantly of saddle soap and leather, glorious smells that all horse lovers appreciate. Along two walls were rows of saddle trees, all labelled but many empty, and bridles, also named, hung above. There was a large desk with several diaries and a cash register on it and behind this a notice board showing a price list as well as some very old and faded photographs and a few tattered rosettes. All emblems of better days, I realized, and I wondered what had been the cause of the sadness and neglect that hung over everything.

I looked away from the notice board and saw that Julia Symonds, coffee mugs in hands, was gazing curiously at me.

'You're not what I expected,' she said abruptly, setting the coffee down on the desk.

'Oh?' A few generations of Henderson arrogance was echoed in the sound. I heard it and for once didn't care. Her saying this proved that my 'disguise' had been a failure. I didn't want questions and enquiries. I wanted my escape, and that happened to be rooted firmly in these stables.

The snub had no effect for she merely grinned good naturedly. 'I'll be honest, Miss Henderson. I've had two other offers for the stables. One I had no hesitation in refusing though the offer was a good one. The other came from a farmer who would have bought the land only and put it under the plough. I would have had to sell the animals separately. You never can tell nowadays — some of them may have ended up at the knacker's yard. I didn't want that. They're good riding school

21

ponies, well-trained, patient, good-tempered. They've worked hard and when they retire they deserve more than to end up in a tin of pet food. Anyway, I'd like the school to continue. It's been my life for almost twenty years and it'll be a wrench to leave.' She sighed and looked round the room, her eyes far away as though she were reliving those long years. Then her eyes sharpened and she looked back at me. 'You're younger than I expected.'

'I know about horses. What has age to do with it?'

'It has to do with experience, the ability to handle and get on with people. All sorts of people, not just the clients but those with horses in livery here — there are fourteen at present and room for more; people buying and selling; the girls who work here and the numerous youngsters that help out; the blacksmith; the vet. There's the teaching itself — there's more to it than just being able to ride yourself, which I presume you can do. Have you taught riding?'

'Yes. I have all the relevant qualifications as I told you in my letter. And I worked for a friend who has a riding school near Preston.' I felt no need to point out that I had helped Janine for fun, when I felt like it, that Daddy had refused point blank to allow me to work there, or that I had been too spineless to fight. Even now I couldn't stand up to him face to face but had to resort to running away to somewhere he would never think of looking for me.

I tried desperately to instil confidence into my next words. 'Miss Symonds, I appreciate that the riding school has been your life for many years and that you are concerned for its future. But perhaps no one would shape up to all your ideas of a perfect successor. At least I love horses and would do my utmost to make a success of the place.'

She suddenly grinned. 'You're probably right. Well, I'll show you round and when you've seen the place maybe you won't want to buy.'

We went outside. The early spring mist still had not cleared completely and it hung thickly over the hills above the stables. A dozen or more horses of assorted sizes and colours grazed there. 'Are they yours?' I asked.

'Grass liveries most of 'em. A few are mine. I haven't needed to use all the animals at once,' she added in an oddly evasive way.

I thought it strange. The riding schools I knew all did booming business, with people often having to book weeks in advance for weekend rides. And as this was the first part of the Easter holidays, all the horses *should* have been required. However, I said nothing, but followed her to the first row of loose boxes.

The long side of the quadrangle consisted, as I had guessed, of a double row of stalls, separated from each other by a narrow concrete walk. The stalls at the rear overlooked a small, enclosed field with a barn partially filled with hay. I looked into the stall where a bay

24

with very intelligent eyes glanced benignly at me from its hay bale. I rubbed his ears and he accepted this as his right, nuzzling lightly at my hand. I gave him a piece of carrot I had brought with me. While he was searching for another piece, the pale girl I had noticed before came along carrying a bucket.

'This is Kirsty Wentworth,' Miss Symonds said, introducing us. 'Kirsty, this is Miss Henderson. She is thinking of buying the stables.'

The girl's face flushed slightly as she smiled. 'Oh, I do hope you do, Miss Henderson. It would be dreadful if the school had to close down.'

She moved on and into a stall farther along. To me Miss Symonds said in a lowered voice: 'She's a very good, hard working girl, and particularly good with beginners. Unfortunately she only works here on a casual basis though I'd like to have her full-time. I have two other paid workers. Diane Fairburn is full-time — unfortunately this is her day off so you won't meet her, and Jenny Cooper who does the weekends. Diane teaches the beginners while I generally concentrate on the more advanced pupils. We take it in turns to supervise the country hacks. I recommend both Jenny and Diane to you if you do decide to buy. Diane is a rather taciturn girl but invaluable. You really can't manage a riding school without at least two helpers.'

I nodded non-committally. 'What about all these other girls?'

'Oh, you'll need them. No riding school could possibly function without all its voluntary helpers. Many of them have a particular horse they take care of — they come here straight from school in the evenings and are here all weekends and school holidays.'

'Untrained?' I asked.

'They learn by watching. Most of them are very good. As I said, no riding school could do without them.'

'I know.' Even Janine, with her most efficiently run riding school, had her young girl helpers. But hers were trained by a series of carefully graded tests of stable and horse management which she had worked out for herself; with each grade reached, a further responsibility was given to the girl until on reaching the fourth grade she was permitted full charge of a horse. There would have to be changes here, I decided at once, but I said nothing of what I was thinking to Miss Symonds. I was half afraid she might change her mind about selling to me if she thought I disapproved of her method of running things. Time enough to make changes when the contracts were signed.

I looked at the woman beside me. 'I've seen everything I need to see. You have my offer and all I need now is your acceptance of it.'

'I'll give you your due,' she replied. 'You know your own mind and I daresay you always get what you want.'

Was that so obvious? I wondered. But then I smiled because actually it wasn't entirely true. I suppose I had always got the material things I asked for, but as I grew older I had discovered that there were other things more desirable — like freedom to choose my own friends and my own way of life.

'Not always,' I said flatly. 'However, I hope to this time. I called in to see a solicitor in Swindon on my way here and he has agreed to act for me. This is his card.'

She took the business card and glanced at it. 'As I said, I've had two other offers but I'm reluctant to accept either of them. I'll be in touch with your solicitor.'

She walked with me back to my car. 'If you want to contact me about anything, I'd appreciate it if you would do so through the solicitor,' I told her. She gave me a swift, suspicious look which I chose to ignore. Whatever happened, I didn't want anything to go amiss with The Plan. I wanted no one at home to remember, in the weeks to come, that I had once received letters with a Salisbury postmark.

2

I stayed the night in an hotel in Salisbury and the next morning, which was a Monday, I drove home, taking my time and missing out the motor-ways altogether, putting off the evil moment when I would arrive home. I grew more apprehensive as I drew northward. I had never been very adept at telling lies and there would be plenty of questions asked about my whereabouts over the last three days. Everyone had assumed I had been visiting an old school friend in Gloucestershire, an assumption I had allowed to grow casually over the past few weeks.

When I drove up to the house I was dismayed, though not surprised, to see Martin's car parked in the drive. I parked beside it and went round the back of the house. Still putting off the evil moment, I thought, self-deprecatingly. The garages were at the rear of the house. Originally they had consisted of stables and a coach house. Now there was room for my car, Daddy's Bentley and his Rover, and the Morris Traveller used as a general runaround by everyone. There was also one real stable at the back, overlooking a small field, where I kept Lady. She was grazing in the field and came straight to my call, nuzzling me with real pleasure. I was struck afresh by her good looks, after seeing the rather pedestrian animals at the riding school. Her dark grey coat was glossy and shone with health, her eyes were bright. I fondled her silky ears and offered her a carrot.

'I don't know how you'll get on down there, sweetheart, but I daresay you're not such a snob that you mind. You'll probably like the company.'

She pushed against me, her breath tickling my neck.

'I hope you don't object, but I took

her out this morning. She badly needed the exercise.'

The voice came from directly behind me. My heart, not to mention my whole body, did a horrible nervous jump that sent Lady snorting away from me. The jump had to do with wondering how long he had been there and how much he had heard of what I said, but was also to do with the mere sound of his voice. I carefully adjusted my expression and turned around.

'She can take your weight well enough,' I said coolly.

He came over and lightly kissed my cheek, the kind of casual, vaguely affectionate greeting we had used for years. He was wearing an open neck shirt and brown cord slacks, and looked every inch the open air, healthy type, which he was, and like a farmer, which he definitely was not. I marvelled anew every time I saw my cousin that anyone could look so handsome, so affable, giving the impression of a lot of fire held in check, but really be so dismally cold blooded.

Martin, whose father had died, leaving him a thriving string of supermarkets with branches in most of the large towns in the north when he was twenty-one, had promptly sold the lot and taken to living the life of a country squire, spending his time hunting, shooting and fishing, or lying on beaches in various fashionable resorts of the world. He had a string of successful investments behind him and had managed, through them, to keep his fortune intact.

'Have a good weekend?' he asked.

'Fine, thanks.'

'You must tell me about it at dinner. Uncle Robert invited me.'

'I expect he did.' I walked towards the house. 'Excuse me, Martin. I think I'll get changed and have an hour's ride before it gets dark. See you later.'

'Sure,' he said, in a bored voice as though he really didn't give a damn where I went or what I did — which he most probably didn't. He let me walk a few paces before calling my name.

'Have you thought about what we discussed on Thursday?'

'I gave you my answer then,' I said levelly. For once I was glad of the cool arrogance in my voice, the tone as bored as his.

'I thought you may have changed your mind.'

'Did you? I can't imagine why.'

His eyes narrowed but I thought with calculation rather than with pique. He leaned back against the fence, his legs crossed at the ankles, elegant, handsome, bored, his eyelids drooping heavily.

'It might be to our mutual advantage,' he said, his cultured accentless voice slowing to a deep drawl. 'We like the same things, know the same people, live the same sort of lives . . . '

Not for long, I thought, but I said, 'Don't you consider we would also bore each other rather effectively?'

He smiled, apparently with real

humour. As smiles went it was quite devastating but I steeled myself to be dispassionate about it. Fortunately I genuinely believed what I had said. It was true that I had loved Martin from about the age of two, that even through brief crushes on other males I had always returned to him, but I did believe that we would bore each other to death. Our relationship was cold and lifeless; even his proposal the previous Thursday had been, in his own words, merely a suggestion that marriage might be to our mutual advantage.

'I'm sure you would never bore me, my sweet,' Martin said, pushing himself off the fence and approaching me. I turned and walked away and he followed, whistling softly. When we arrived at the house he added, 'I think it only fair to tell you that I mentioned it to Uncle Robert and he thoroughly approves.'

'He would,' I retorted. 'But as it's not he who would have to marry you, his opinion doesn't count.'

He put out one hand and lightly flicked a strand of hair back from my face. 'There's no one else, is there? No love-lorn swain with an eye on the Henderson fortune?'

I dragged away from him. He had caught hold of the lock of hair and as I jerked back, his fingers tightened. The pain brought a rush of tears to my eyes and I turned quickly so that he should not see. I came at that moment as near to hating him as I ever had.

★　★　★

In twenty minutes I had changed into jeans and riding boots and was astride Lady's back, cantering through the nearby woods. I was choked and angry with what Martin had said but honest enough to admit that his comments were not entirely unjustified. I was attractive but looks were comparatively unimportant when one was the only daughter of Robert Henderson. It had happened enough times — the apparently genuine young man, perhaps moderately wealthy, the son of one of Daddy's acquaintances, perhaps relatively penniless. And always there had been the doubts. I was very sure of my own worth in everything but in my power to attract a man for myself. If I married Martin, at least I would know he didn't want me for my money. He had quite enough of that himself.

But I wasn't going to marry Martin. I was going to run away in a highly cowardly fashion, to a place where no one had ever heard of Robert Henderson save, perhaps, on the financial pages of their newspapers. I let Lady walk slowly home on a loose rein, her neck stretched and head lowered, and managed a faint smile. I could afford to smile now because there was an escape for me — Hillcroft Riding School where no one would know anything about me other than what I allowed them to know.

Daddy was predictably surprised that

I was going to sell Lady but assumed I had at last grown out of what he considered a silly and wasteful passion for horses, and would now turn to more sensible things. Martin, equally predictably, was even more surprised and extremely cynical.

'I suppose it's because you've never got farther than the local shows with her,' he drawled. It was the same evening; we had had dinner and coffee and now I was eating my way through a plateful of after-dinner mints while Daddy and Martin drank brandy and smoked cigars. Very pleasant, very civilized. I was glad they couldn't read my thoughts which were neither pleasant nor civilized. 'The old adage about a bad workman blaming his tools is right, you know. The reason you haven't got further is because of you, not the mare.'

'I'm surprised you know anything at all about such plebian articles as *tools*, Martin,' I said sweetly and he acknowledged the comment with a grin. 'As it happens, a friend of mine has offered a good price for Lady and I'm selling her.'

The friend was Sarah-Jane Markham, an old school friend who lived about fifteen miles away. She would take delivery of Lady, keep her for a few weeks and then her husband would drive the mare south and deliver her to the Hillcroft Riding School. It all seemed unnecessarily complicated but was the only way I could think of to keep Lady without revealing my plans. Martin gave me a sudden sharp look as though he had guessed things were not what they seemed, then he shrugged slightly, his shoulders moving in an almost Gallic way beneath the mohair dinner jacket.

'I don't know why there has to be an inquest!' I snapped. 'Lady is mine and I can do what I like with her!'

'After all the fuss you made about having her,' Daddy grunted, seeming to come out of a reverie. 'Still, it's just as well. You won't have time for all that nonsense when you are married.'

There was a little awkward pause. My father, despite being a very tough, hard headed business man, was adept at ignoring what he didn't want to see. Martin's eyes met mine; his were ironically amused, mine defiant. He finished his brandy and placed the glass on the table.

'I thought I told you, sir, that Lindsay turned me down.'

Daddy looked between us. 'What? Nonsense! You know what girls are like. I suppose you didn't approach the subject properly. In my days a young fellow thought a lot about how to make a proposal.'

Martin grinned. 'I don't think going down on one knee and declaring my undying devotion would actually have helped. She thinks we'll bore each other to death.'

The mint I was eating tasted suddenly bitter. I swallowed it and stood up. 'I have more important things to do than to sit listening to all this nonsense. I've said I don't want to marry Martin and I mean it. When I do get married it'll be because I want to and not because you two seem to think it will be a good idea!'

I left the room to the sound of Martin's loud burst of laughter.

★　★　★

Sarah-Jane and her husband Scott, lived in a cottage in the village of Upper Lascombe. Scott was a freelance writer who did a lot of work for television and both he and Sarah-Jane were unconventional to the extreme. I had no trouble at all in recruiting their help in my escape. Scott in particular was rather heavily left wing and believed that people like my father should be set down as often as possible, and if helping me did one thing to thwart Robert Henderson, Scott would do it. Sarah-Jane wanted to help simply because she was my friend and because she knew how I felt about the escape.

'We've fixed up the shed at the back for Lady,' she told me, leading me to the rear of the cottage. 'It isn't very big but it's clean and there's a small field. It'll only be for a couple of weeks anyway, won't it?'

'Yes. I won't bring her over until the contracts are signed and I have a definite date for moving.' I looked at the shed and pronounced it suitable, then we went inside and drank coffee in the kitchen. The tapping from Scott's typewriter came from upstairs where he had his study.

'Tell me about the riding school,' Sarah-Jane said comfortably. 'Obviously you found it to your liking.'

I nodded. 'It's a bit run down but that doesn't matter. In fact I don't want a business that is running smoothly. I want something that needs to be worked at. I got the impression that things haven't been going too well for Miss Symonds, the present owner. There must be something in the region of twenty-five horses and ponies there yet only half of them were being used, and that at a weekend, too. Yet there are several villages about and Salisbury is only four miles away.'

'Perhaps there are other riding schools.'

'There are, of course, but the area is large enough to support more than one. I looked in the telephone directory and the nearest is six miles away. I really don't think that should make much difference.'

'I expect you'll soon sort things out,' Sarah-Jane said, with a touching confidence in my ability. We had gone to a very exclusive girls' public school together, she having been sent there by a wealthy aunt, for the fees would have been far beyond the means of her parents. At first she had been lost and out of place, a timid little thing who had roused my protective instincts. After a few months she had blossomed out and no longer needed my protection — in fact, in our final year she became head girl while I could achieve no higher than House Captain. But those first few months had served to put a firm seal on our friendship.

'Do you mind if I start bringing my things over bit by bit?' I asked her. 'I can't leave the house with all that I want to take in one go — it would really give the game away. There's clothes of course, and books, and all my records, as well as one or two bigger things like a couple of pictures and my portable television set. Then there are some odd bits and pieces of harness that might come in useful. I thought that if I brought the stuff over a bit at a time no one would notice. There would be room for it all in the horsebox when Scott drives Lady down to Wiltshire.'

'Yes, of course,' she said easily, pouring more coffee. 'But Lindsay, what are you going to say to your father? You'll have to explain something or he'd surely call the police. Anyway, it wouldn't be fair to worry him.'

'I realize that. I thought I'd leave a note saying I was safe and well, something like that, but not actually giving him any information. It'll be just enough to stop him calling the police. He may do that still, especially as he's friendly with the Chief Constable, but the local force is undermanned and I can't see them feeling justified in putting themselves out looking for someone who doesn't want to be found.'

'What about Martin?' Sarah-Jane asked.

'*What* about Martin?'

'We . . . ll, I thought you and he . . . that he . . . ' She hesitated and blushed slightly. 'Sorry, Lindsay. I don't suppose it's any of my business but you did tell me ages ago how you felt about Martin so I wondered . . . '

If she had been anyone else I might well have uttered something thoroughly snubbing for I have always hated anyone probing into my private life. But what she said was true — I *had* once told her of my feelings for Martin. She was the only person who did know.

Besides, she was helping me and as such deserved some answers.

'You don't understand,' I began slowly, 'how it feels to be given everything you ask for in life except the right to choose and to live the life you want. You and Scott — you have so much freedom. I know you're sometimes short of money but, God, there are worse things.' I smiled at her expression. '*And* I know it's easy for me to say that — but it's true! I found out the hard way. I'm sick of being Robert Henderson's daughter, and if I married Martin I would be Robert Henderson's daughter who is married to Martin Henderson. Big deal. Martin thinks our marriage would be advantageous to both of us. Can you imagine being proposed to because it's advantageous?'

'But you said you love him.'

'I *do*! But I don't want him on those terms. I'll cope without him far better than I would be able to cope married to him. There's a lot of work to be done at the riding school and that's what I need.'

Sarah-Jane sighed and opened her brown eyes very wide. 'Are you sure you know what you want, Lindsay?'

'Yes,' I said with conviction. 'For the first time in my life I do know. I want Hillcroft Riding School. I want to make a success of it without the help of my father. And I want to meet people on equal terms, not being looked upon as some kind of freak but as an ordinary person.'

For a moment, as I said this, I seemed to hear a cold, masculine voice saying: 'You're a spoiled, ill-mannered brat who probably deserves a bloody good spanking.' If I wanted to be treated as an ordinary person I would have to try very hard to leave the old Lindsay Henderson behind me.

3

At the beginning of May, driving a four-year-old Ford Escort estate that I had bought in a garage in Swindon, I arrived at Wickham, which was the village closest to the riding school and from there drove straight to the school. The previous week I had gone down to Swindon and there, in the office of the solicitor I had found on my previous visit, I signed the contract which made me the official owner of the Hillcroft Riding School, its land and stock complete. Miss Symonds was also present; we talked a little about the stables and she agreed to stay on until I got there so that the changing of hands would be a smooth operation. She would, she told me, cancel all rides and lessons for the first few days so that I would have time to settle in and sort myself out before starting properly.

At the same time I had taken over the lease of the tiny, two bedroom cottage presently occupied by Miss Symonds. The final part of The Plan was put into operation the following day when Scott Markham drove Lady to Hillcroft. He reported that before leaving her he had seen her safely installed in one of the many looseboxes.

I left Daddy a note, not extensive, certainly not explanatory, sufficient, as I told Sarah-Jane, to prevent him from calling out the police, though I still wouldn't have put that past him. I told him not to try to find me as I had no intention of returning home to live, but that sometime in the future I would get in touch. It wasn't a satisfactory letter and I made out many drafts before settling for one. It was suddenly harder than I had expected to pull up my roots and drive away from the house I had known all my life. Until then I had enjoyed the subterfuge as though it were a game, the little pantomime over Lady, the secreting of my belongings over to Sarah-Jane's cottage; arranging for my bank account to be transferred to a branch in Southampton because I had no great faith in the discretion of our local bank manager who, like many of the business people around, was scared to death of my father. I intended putting up with the inconvenience of having a bank in Southampton for a little while then transferring the whole of my account to another, different bank in Salisbury.

All this covering of my traces had been fun but half way on the final journey south I suffered a bad attack of nerves. Cold feet were nothing to the panic I felt. It was not too late, I reasoned. I could turn round and go straight home and no one would be any the wiser. After all, suppose everything went wrong. I had a good deal of money, money left to me by my mother as my own to do with as I wished — she, too, had suffered from Daddy's dominant personality — money made from the sale of the Italian sports car, money saved from a generous allowance over the past years. But if the riding school was not a success, if it continued on the downward path it was evidently on at this moment, that money would not last long. Suppose I had to admit my failure and go home? All right, I could ride quite well and I had the bit of paper that said I was a qualified British Horse Society Assistant Riding Instructor, but I began to realize I had no more idea about the ordinary, every day running of stables with twenty odd horses in than a five-year-old did. Whether I liked it or not I couldn't be entirely independent at first. I would have to rely on those girls who worked for Miss Symonds.

All these thoughts were lowering and frightening. Later I was ashamed of how near I had come to giving up before I had even started. I told myself sternly that if I gave up now someone *would* know, *I* would know. For the rest of my life I would be ashamed of myself and my cowardice. I had to go on.

It was early afternoon when I drove through the small village of Wickham and headed towards the stables. I had found another way to reach them that did not involve taking the same narrow muddy lane, so that there was no repeat encounter with an irate farmer to mar my arrival. The weather was glorious, as days in May can be; the hedgerows were bright with hawthorn blossom, young leaves glowed in thousands of shades of soft green and the ponies in the fields looked sleek and healthy and fit. My earlier doubts and fears faded. I turned the Escort into the gate and drove across the yard to park it in the clearing beyond.

Miss Symond's Land Rover was still there with a horsebox attached and she was there herself, in the process of leading the ugly dun horse into it with the help of a thin dark girl I had not seen before. I got out of the car and watched, and when the horse was safely shut in, Miss Symonds came over to me.

'Welcome to Hillcroft', she said with a smile, and we shook hands. 'All ready, are you?'

'I hope so,' I grinned. 'Is Lady all right?'

'The grey mare? Yes, she's fine. A lovely animal, excellent breeding, I should say, and very goodmannered. Must have cost you a pretty packet.'

'Yes,' I agreed non-committally, sensing her curiosity. I glanced towards the dark girl who was looking steadily at me. Miss Symonds introduced her as Diane Fairburn and I remembered her saying that she had a full time helper called Diane. She was a thin-faced, sullen looking girl who would have been quite attractive if she had made more of herself. Her long, almost black hair was tied back with an elastic band and her complexion was roughened and sun tanned. I wasn't at all sure that I cared for the narrow eyed way she stared at me but I was prepared to hold my opinion for a while. Miss Symonds didn't strike me as the kind of person who would employ someone who didn't pull their weight.

'There's not much for you to do this evening,' Miss Symonds was saying. 'All the evening feeds are ready and the grass liveries have been fed. You can relax a bit on your first evening.' I smiled my thanks for this thoughtfulness and she continued: 'I've moved all my stuff out of the cottage. In fact, I'm all ready to go.' She glanced round the yard, her expression suddenly melancholy. 'I'll . . . I'll just take a last look round.'

I left her to it for she obviously wanted to say goodbye in her own way. We were both beginning something new, she in her little cottage by the sea, me in this new undertaking. It was a sobering thought that neither of us knew for certain how we would be able to cope with our change of circumstances.

Then I realized that Diane Fairburn had not moved but was leaning in a curiously insolent fashion against the tack room door staring at me, her hands thrust into the back pockets of her jeans. Until then she had said nothing other than a brief 'Hello,' when we were introduced. Now she said:

'She doesn't want to leave. She belongs here — she's lived in Wickham over thirty years and had the school for eighteen of them.'

I wasn't quite sure how to reply to what sounded almost like censure. 'I suppose after so long she'll be glad of the rest.'

'I don't know about that,' the girl muttered in a peculiarly spiteful way. 'Don't know what she'll do in a silly little cottage by the sea. She loves this place.'

She turned away as she spoke, tossing her head so that the black pony tail jerked. 'Why is she leaving then?' I demanded and she half turned back.

'She couldn't take it any longer, that's why . . . all the bad luck. Do you think you'll last? The school's losing money hand over fist. You might as well sell out now before you lose too much.'

She walked away from me, into the tack room. I watched her a moment, thoughtful, then followed her. She was sitting on the stool by the desk flicking through the pages of a magazine that lay there. I thought she was merely trying to look busy.

I didn't ask her what it was that Miss Symonds couldn't take any longer, or what she meant by 'bad luck', because that seemed to have been said simply from a sense of melodrama. She looked the kind of girl who liked to be in the centre of things. I had had a friend at school like that, a French girl who liked nothing better than to relate some highly improbable tale to an enthralled audience. It was years before we discovered that most of what she said was due to a highly active imagination.

However, I did ask: 'To whom should I sell?'

She looked up quickly. 'Miss Symonds had two other offers for the school. I don't know why she decided to sell to you.'

And you won't be very long in a job, my girl, if you carry on talking to me like that, I thought, but I merely said, mildly enough: 'She told me. For some reason she wouldn't talk about the first offer she had except to say that she disapproved of the person who made the offer and wouldn't contemplate selling to him. The other was a farmer who intended putting the land under the plough.'

'That's Alan Wentworth,' she said quickly. 'He wants the land very badly. He is very annoyed with Miss Symonds because she refused to sell to him.'

'That's entirely up to her, isn't it?' I reminded her coolly. 'She wants Hillcroft to continue as a riding school and knew that I would be making quite sure of that.' I turned away and on second thoughts, glanced back at her. I piled every ounce of arrogance and hauteur into my voice and posture. 'I shall be spending the rest of today sorting out the cottage. Please be here early tomorrow morning as I shall be wanting to discuss the future running of the stables.'

She failed to be impressed though her eyes widened a little. 'It's all the same to me,' she shrugged. 'I've had plenty of offers of other jobs. I'm not at all sure that I want to stay here anyway, not once Julia's gone.'

'Then I suggest you make up your mind and let me know as soon as possible,' I told her sharply. 'I really don't intend wasting my time with reluctant workers.'

I marched out of the tack room feeling grimly that I had not taken many minutes to make myself an enemy. Diane Fairburn had looked fit to do murder at that moment. She obviously had held up the other job offers as a threat, little realizing I would react as I had. I was not particularly bothered. If she did decide to leave it would be a bit of a nuisance having to find another full-time worker but I hadn't liked Diane much and didn't think we would get on well together.

Miss Symonds had finished her final tour. I went with her to her Land Rover and watched her get in and start up the engine. 'I had all your belongings put into the cottage,' she told me before driving off. 'I'm afraid you may find the cottage rather dull and gloomy but structurally it's sound and that's the main thing. And it is an advantage living right beside the stables. Goodbye, my dear, and good luck.'

★   ★   ★

When I first came to look at the riding school I hadn't bothered to inspect the cottage and that, I soon discovered, had been a great mistake for if I had there was no way I would have contemplated living in it. Structurally sound it might have been though I had my doubts about that; anyway it was dingy and dark and not outstanding for its cleanliness. The garden, small in front, vast in the rear, was overgrown and the windows were so filthy that only the merest flicker of daylight penetrated into the small beamed rooms. I thought of Miss Symonds with her weary, good natured face, her tatty clothes and neglected appearance and realized that the cottage was a reflection of her. I stood in the tiny hall, smelling the damp fustiness, and firmly put behind me all thoughts of the beautiful home I had left for this. The cottage had possibilities; it needed only hard work to sort it out. I would go into Salisbury and buy white paint, lashings of it. I would paint everything white except the lovely oak beams that stretched across the living room ceiling; I would get pretty new curtains to hang at the windows, have a stainless steel sink unit put in to replace the awful chipped enamel one at present in the kitchen, and a new electric stove instead of the very ancient gas one. In the meantime I would clean up the kitchen, bathroom and one bedroom, and that would do for the present.

Fortunately there was an immersion heater. I would have been completely thrown by a solid fuel burning stove. I turned on the heater and walked down to the village shop to get some cleaning materials. It was latish afternoon by then and the pleasant May evening, though chilly, held a promise of more lovely days to come. I consoled myself with the thought that it might have been raining, also that people might have been less friendly.

The walk to the shop took about ten minutes; I had to go down the lane I had driven down before, which led to the one main street of Wickham village, and the shop was near. It was one of those typical village stores containing a post office, but all its stock was sold on what amounted to a self service system. The post mistress and the lady at the check out till, both so alike that they must have been sisters, eyed me with great and open curiosity as did the only customer but no one said more than to reply to my 'Good afternoon', until I was on my way out, then the customer, a very elderly woman with a friendly enough face, touched my arm.

'You'd be the one who's bought Hillcroft?' she suggested, and I nodded.

'Yes. I'm Lindsay Henderson.'

'Oh, yes? Well, good luck to you, my dear,' she said, unconsciously echoing Julia Symond's words. I smiled and thanked her, and went out, pulling the door to behind me though not before I heard one of the other women saying:

'She'll need that good luck, Ruby. If Julia Symonds couldn't cope with all that bad luck I don't know how a little sprig of a thing like that can do it. You know about the curse on the place.'

I was thoughtful as I walked back to the cottage. Diane Fairburn had talked of Hillcroft being beset by bad luck, the woman in the shop said 'all that bad luck'. Though of course the other reference to a curse was nonsense, I had myself felt that the riding school was more run down than it should have been. My solicitor had looked into it and told me it wasn't a very profitable enterprise though until a year or so ago it had made a small profit. He had attempted to dissuade me from buying for he could not understand that my primary interest was not in making a vast profit. Still, I didn't want to run into debt or be forced to dip deeper into my capital. I wanted the school to be a going concern and all this talk of bad luck was scarcely reassuring.

But there's nothing like hard physical work for dispelling the miseries. Soon, up to my elbows in soapy water, I was so busy scrubbing floors and walls, washing paintwork, attacking cobwebs and cleaning windows that I had no time to worry about the things I had heard. After a couple of hours it was nearly dark and my back and arms ached abominably. I was unused to housework of any description, though I *had* done such menial tasks before. My maternal grandmother was a great one for doing her own spring cleaning and often as a girl I had gone to stay with her in her cottage in Hertfordshire to help her. It had been fun to put all the furniture, one room at a time, out on to the lawn, actually to beat the rugs over the washing line, wash the covers and curtains and really give the rooms a going over before moving the furniture back inside. All by hand, too — no washing machines and vacuum cleaners for my Grandmama! It was good oldfashioned spring cleaning that most likely did not get done these days. Certainly these rooms didn't look as though they had seen spring cleaning in many a long year, but at the end of two hours, at least the kitchen was clean and fit to be used, and I was just thinking rather wearily about the bedroom when the door was tapped.

It was the pretty, pale faced girl called Kirsty whom I had met before. Despite the mild evening she wore a thick jumper over jeans and her face seemed paler than I remembered, but her smile was warm and welcoming.

'I thought I'd come and see how you were coping,' she said. 'I know what a dreadful state the cottage was in. Julia hated housework and never did any if she could help it. Oh, you've done wonders in here!' I had taken her through into the kitchen. 'You must have worked hard.'

'Yes, but it's all I've done. I was just thinking about tackling a bedroom. Still, your coming has given me a good excuse to stop for coffee. Sit down and I'll make some.'

I switched on the percolator and while I fetched cups, milk and sugar Kirsty talked about Lady, whom she had looked at when she arrived two days earlier. She spoke in a quick, rather breathless manner and I felt all the time that she really had something far more important to talk about than commonplaces about the stable and horses. It finally came out, as we were finishing our coffee and I was facing the thought of more cleaning.

'I met Diane Fairburn earlier,' she

said in a rush. 'She told me she might not be staying with you. Is that true?'

'I really don't know,' I said with a smile. 'She told me she had been offered another job and it seemed to me she wanted to leave but it was left a bit in the air. I'll have to wait and see. I don't think we'd get on very well together so perhaps it would be as well if she did leave.'

'Diane can be a bit . . . difficult,' Kirsty murmured, fiddling about in an embarrassed way with her coffee cup. 'Did she say what the other job was?'

'No — and I didn't ask.'

'Oh . . . ' There was another long silence and I grinned, suddenly understanding.

'You wouldn't by any chance be looking for a full-time job?' I asked. 'I really could do with another helper.'

She looked up, an expression of real joy on her face, and a bit of colour flooded into her cheeks.

'Oh, yes! You wouldn't . . . I mean, I sort of hoped you'd consider . . . I do want to work full-time and it would be marvellous to work at Hillcroft. It's so difficult to get a job out here; you see if I worked in town the bus fares are so extortionate that it hardly seems worthwhile. I'm not qualified to teach riding though, but I've helped Julia before.'

'I know, she told me. And as long as I'm qualified I don't think it matters that you're not.' I laughed at her evident joy. 'I didn't think you'd be so eager. It's going to be very hard work especially over the next few months. The stables are awfully run down and I have loads of new ideas that you may not approve of. You really want to take it on?'

She nodded. 'More than anything. It will be marvellous. I asked Julia often but she used to say Diane was enough, and Jenny at the weekends. Besides, Julia and Diane were very pally and I felt a bit out of it. Diane is my brother's girlfriend — or thinks she is anyway — and she's often at home. She can be catty and unpleasant to me. I don't know what Alan sees in her — she's a very underhand sort of girl.'

The name of Alan Wentworth suddenly rang a chord in my memory. I frowned, puzzled, then remembered. 'Diane told me it was an Alan Wentworth who wanted to buy Hillcroft, a farmer who wanted the land.'

Kirsty nodded. 'That's my brother. He did make an offer to Julia though I don't think he really expected her to accept it. But the land would have been useful and it would have been better than if Matthew Lawson had bought the stables.' Her face brightened into a radiant smile. 'It was wonderful when we heard that someone else altogether had bought Hillcroft and intended keeping it as a riding school.'

'Who is Matthew Lawson?'

'Oh — ' she seemed to hesitate, frowning a little. 'Don't you know about him? I thought Julia might have mentioned him.'

'She said she had another offer but was very reluctant to talk about it. I got the impression she didn't at all like the person who made the offer and wouldn't even contemplate selling to him.'

'Yes, that would be Matthew Lawson. I know Julia hated him. He lives round here now but comes from the Midlands somewhere. He isn't a bit countrified and I can't imagine what he wants the stables for. Apparently he's filthy rich and offered Julia a huge amount for the stables. I'm so glad she turned him down and wasn't influenced by the money. I really can't stand people who think everything has its price.'

'Nor me,' I agreed, thinking ruefully of my own father who was certainly one such person. However, I didn't want to think too seriously about that so I glanced at my watch and said: 'I had better go and make one last check on the horses. Will you come?'

'Of course,' she said promptly. 'I looked in on the way over and everything was okay. Diane may be a prize bitch but she is very efficient.'

I said nothing about her vocabulary which was, after all, nothing to do with me and might well be accurate anyway. We checked on the horses, all now either in their stables or out in the field, fed and settled happily, and I told Kirsty about my plans for some kind of graded test for the children who helped in the riding school. She showed guarded enthusiasm. I would have asked her for a more honest opinion but I noticed then that as she went to each stable she tested the door.

'Why are you doing that?'

She seemed surprised, as though she had been doing it without realizing she was. 'I don't know. We had a few cases of doors not being locked properly. Julia was always on about it. We had a pony once who used to jump over the stable door but this was different for the doors were actually left open. And once someone left the gate to the field open and eight of the ponies got out into the lane. Luckily we managed to catch most of them before any damage was done but one panicked and ran into a parked car; the poor thing hurt itself so badly it had to be put down. The car driver played merry hell of course and the whole thing didn't do the school's reputation much good.'

'I can imagine. Did Miss Symonds ever find out who left the gate open?'

'No one would admit it. It was probably an accident, just bad luck.'

Just bad luck — one of those bursts of bad luck I had heard about. 'An old lady in the village shop said the stable had a curse on it,' I said slowly, and Kirsty burst into hearty laughter.

'That'll be Mrs Gresham, I bet. She loves spreading gloom and despondency. It all started a couple of years ago when some gypsies tried to settle on part of Julia's land and she had them run off. Someone, just for a joke, said they would put a curse on Julia and silly old things like Mrs Gresham took it up.'

'You don't believe in it then?'

'Of course not. Who believes in

curses these days?'

'But Miss Symonds did have bad luck?'

'Well ... yes. But that was just coincidence. I think a lot of the things that went wrong recently were due to carelessness. Over the last few months Julia really hasn't had much heart for the stables. She had appendicitis last year and after that never seemed to get back the same enthusiasm. You can see how run down everything is and we've lost a lot of customers because she didn't seem to care as much as she used to.'

While we were talking, leaning against the wall near Lady's stall, Diane had joined us. I noticed that Kirsty gave her a quick, uncertain look during this last speech, which was soon explained by Diane's fiery repudiation of it.

'That's not true, Kirsty! How can you say such things! Julia loved the stables. It wasn't carelessness, all the things that went wrong — it was bad luck.'

'You don't believe in this gypsy curse?' I asked incredulously and she shook her head, but looked mulishly stubborn.

'I don't know what I believe,' she muttered, turning away. 'But it'll be interesting to see if it goes on, won't it?'

We watched her walk across the yard to where a couple of bicycles were leaning against the wall. I glanced at Kirsty who raised her eyebrows comically, but I decided it was prudent not to discuss Diane.

'Tell me about this bad luck,' I said instead. 'Apart from the horses getting out, what else happened?'

'Oh, last summer the hay rick caught fire. Julia wasn't well insured and having to buy another load of hay hit her badly. Another time some yobs — criminal, stupid louts — broke into the tack room one night when everyone had gone home. When we came in next morning we found all the tack in a heap on the floor. The saddles had been slashed and the bridles broken, and red paint had been tipped over the lot. It was terrible.'

'That wasn't just carelessness!' I protested, horrified.

'Of course not. Though Julia admitted she had forgotten to switch on the burglar alarm and more than once I had come in early and found she hadn't locked the tack room door. The police never found out who did it but there are a couple of Hell's Angel type gangs round here and it may have been one or other of them. They ride their motor bikes up near where we go for the country rides, practising stunts and things, but as far as I know they always behave well towards the horses, cutting their engines when we come near and so on . . . but, well, you never know with that sort.'

What she had told me was hardly reassuring. I thought hard about it all as I finished cleaning up a bedroom and finally, dead tired, crawled into the hard, narrow little bed. I didn't exactly blame Julia Symonds for keeping from me her run of bad luck but it hadn't made very good listening. I didn't believe in the curse either but I decided I'd have to be doubly careful that the bad luck didn't come to me.

4

With the morning my fears seemed foolish and unwarranted. Suddenly, with the sun shining, the cottage looked more habitable by the minute and with the benefit a good night's sleep can give I felt refreshed and ready to begin my new life. I was up early, dressed myself warmly in jeans and sweater and went to start work in the stables where I was surprised and pleased to find Kirsty and Diane there already, measuring out the feed with the help of two girls who apparently came every morning before school. Because the usual rides and lessons had been cancelled this week, many of the animals were turned out into the fields, no doubt a well earned holiday for all of them, and I told the girls to pass the word that I wanted to meet as many as possible of them that evening at five.

'I won't keep you from your home-work,' I told them. 'The meeting won't last more than about half an hour. I want to meet you all and tell you my plans.'

At this point Diane told me that Thursday was usually her day off but that she had decided not to take it today because I was bound to need the help. Not surprisingly, this got my back up so much that I told her she could have the day off willingly and that Kirsty and I could manage perfectly well. As she cycled out of the yard she threw me a sneering look that showed what she thought of my ability to cope with anything. I looked away from her and saw Kirsty watching me. I grinned reluctantly.

'Should I have given her the sack? She really gets my back up.'

Kirsty shrugged. 'It's just her way, and you might find you need her. She *does* know the stables inside out and it's a lot of work for two people.' She shrugged again. 'But it's up to you, of course.'

'Well, I won't be rushed into anything. I'll give it a week or two. Meanwhile, you and I will just have to work harder today. At least I think the atmosphere will be more friendly without her.'

We got down to the necessary jobs of mucking out and tack cleaning. It was a lot of work for two people and would be even more so next week when the horses would need to be brought in, groomed daily, and the lessons and rides organized. Until I had a replacement I really couldn't afford to fall out with Diane whatever the temptation to do so. By lunch time I was feeling as tired as I had the previous evening though it was a different kind of tiredness, much more pleasant. Kirsty however, looked very, very tired and when I finally stopped to think about lunch I was dismayed. Her evident enthusiasm had caused me to forget that she did not seem physically strong.

'I think you've had enough, Kirsty,' I told her, quite frightened to see her pale face and dark, smudged eyes. I led her to the tack room. 'We'll have a cup of tea then you can go home.'

She pushed the two cats, Lucy and Tigger, off one of the very battered armchairs and sank gratefully into it. 'There's plenty more to be done,' she murmured.

'Nothing that I can't do myself, and a lot of the girls are coming after school. This afternoon I thought I'd take Lady out for a ride anyway. I want to have a good look at the countryside around. Miss Symonds left me some maps of the routes she usually took and I'd like to suss them out before I decide which ones I'll use. I'll go about half past two so if you feel up to it come back and ride with me. But I think you should go home and rest, get something to eat and put your feet up.'

She reddened. 'I do feel a bit knocked out, I must admit. There isn't normally so much to do — it's just that nothing much seems to have been done at all over the last week. That tack was filthy.' I had noticed that myself. It seemed to me that Julia Symonds had done as little as possible once she knew I was coming or, conversely, that Diane Fairburn had shirked her duties. That, on the face of it, seemed most likely.

Later, after going back to the cottage for a quick snack of soup and bread roll, I went to the tack room and started to check out the various items there. Most of the stuff was in a reasonable condition and quite a lot was new, presumably because of the vandalism of the previous year. It was a sunny afternoon so I went and sat on the mounting block outside and began the soothing job of soaping one of the scruffier saddles. I was still occupied with this particular job when the peace of the afternoon was interrupted by the advent of a dark blue Range Rover that drove into the yard. I was not averse to being disturbed as cleaning tack was not one of my favourite jobs but the welcome smile that had begun to cross my face, as I prepared to greet a potential client, slipped drastically when I saw the identity of the man at the wheel.

It was my protagonist of the tractor and trailer. I suppose in a way I had expected that at some time or other I might come across him again, for country communities are far more insular than are town ones, but I hadn't expected it to be so soon or that I should actually have a visit from the man. I got to my feet, slowly wiping my hands on the seat of my jeans, and waited while he got out of the vehicle and came towards me. The fact that he was evidently not surprised to see me made me consider that he already knew it was I who had bought the riding school.

'So it *is* you,' he said in a slow, casual voice. 'I guessed it might be.'

'But hoped it wouldn't be,' I added, equally casually. 'Is there something you want? As you can see, I'm busy.'

His eyes narrowed a little. They were blue; not brilliant blue, cornflower blue, or sea blue, but the cold blue-grey of an angry winter's sky. He had a rugged, craggy face that some women would consider attractive, and untidy fair hair. The look he gave me was as contemptuous as I hoped was the one I gave him. He was wearing blue cords and a denim shirt with the sleeves rolled up to the elbows. The appearance was of a big, powerful, outdoor man, physical and rough and not given to caring much about the niceties of life. As I had noticed before, however, the whole appearance was belied by the pleasant cultured voice when he spoke.

'There are a good many things I might want to ask,' he said. 'Like what the hell is someone like you doing taking over Julia Symonds' problems.'

'And I might reply that I'm trying to earn a living.'

'You don't look as though you need ever to earn a living,' he said sneeringly.

'My financial situation has nothing whatsoever to do with you, Mr . . . whatever-your-name-is,' I said childishly.

'The name is Wentworth.'

'Oh!'

Kirsty's brother. I thought about that facer for a moment. They didn't look much alike, Kirsty being slender and frail looking and very gentle. I said, because I was annoyed and because this whole situation had come crashing upon me unawares: 'You're not much like your sister. Obviously when all the charm and friendliness was handed out in your family, she got it all.'

'I can assure you that the good opinion of someone like you is totally unimportant to me,' he said coldly. 'And I didn't come to exchange insults. I came merely to tell you that my sister will no longer be working for you.'

I opened my mouth then closed it again. He stood a moment looking at me, then turned away. I shouted: 'What the hell do you mean? Kirsty was over the moon about working here. Did she tell you she didn't want to work here? Because I don't believe it.'

He turned round, his chest heaving

as in exasperation. Then he came back to me, treading firmly and determinedly. Despite myself I felt intimidated though I fervently hoped this fact was not evident.

'No, she didn't tell me. But I'm telling *you*. Anyone with an ounce of sense would have realized that she isn't up to this kind of work.'

'That's nonsense,' I snapped. 'Admittedly she was tired but we've been working hard. She told me you had brought her up. You're being over protective, Mr Wentworth. Your sister is nineteen and I'm sure quite capable of making up her own mind about whether or not she wishes to work.' I turned away from the gathering fury in his eyes, picked up the saddle I had been working on and headed for the tack room. 'The job is Kirsty's for as long as she wants it,' I retorted over one shoulder.

I had taken two steps into the tack room when my arm was grabbed, I was spun round so hard that I dropped the saddle in my fright. 'Now listen to me, you beautiful little bitch,' Alan Wentworth hissed at me, his fingers gripping my upper arms so that they hurt even through my thick jumper. 'My sister is not strong, and I'm damned if I'm going to stand around while someone like you walks in and encourages her to wreck her health still further.'

It would have been easy to give in; I can't say I wasn't tempted. There was a scarcely suppressed fury in him that I felt in the hands on my arms and saw in the expression on his face. I had never been talked to in such a manner in the whole of my life and it was an experience I had no wish to repeat. For the life of me I couldn't speak and after a few seconds I was released. He straightened, flexing his fingers. I got the fleeting impression that his behaviour had surprised him as much as it had me.

'You seem to think everything can be solved by brute force, Mr Wentworth,' I managed to say, quite sweetly. 'You're bigger than me and no doubt you can fling me about without much effort. But it won't make me change my mind. I know how it feels to be smothered in cotton wool by a stupid man who seems to think women can't do anything for themselves. And I'm about to prove I can look after myself. Why don't you let Kirsty do the same?'

'Because,' he said briefly, before turning on his heels and marching out, 'you, for all your apparent femininity and fragility, are evidently hard as nails, and Kirsty is not.'

It wasn't at all bad as a parting shot and probably was far more of an insult than he realized. There are very few women anywhere, despite what they may say, who like to be considered hard as nails and I certainly wasn't one of them. I wanted to be independent certainly, liberated, free to choose my own life, but hard as nails? No. Besides, I wasn't. After Alan Wentworth had made his angry exit I could cheerfully have sat down and howled. I had been feeling happy and optimistic but these hopeful emotions were now replaced by tiredness and depression. Why, of all people, had the number one MCP to be Kirsty's brother? I did not want to lose Kirsty. I had felt in her an affinity, a comradeship that I felt sure I would need in my first few difficult days at Hillcroft. I wondered if her brother's strength of character would overcome her much more gentle determination to work at the stables.

I tried to drag myself out of this mood by tacking up Lady and riding out to follow one of the sketch maps Julia Symonds had given me. The route I chose took us on a very pleasant ride up through the woods that surrounded Wickham on three sides. I kept to the main track on that occasion but there were numerous side tracks going off through the trees, many of them well worn by untold numbers of horse shoes. I would need to learn all these rides and very quickly though for a little while I could take Diane or Kirsty with me on the hacks.

On the way back I heard the roar of motor bike engines in the distance and through the trees I thought I glimpsed movement as of a vehicle climbing a steep and muddy track. The boys Kirsty had told me about, I presumed, practising their dirt track racing. They were some distance away and the noise did not disturb Lady at all, though her ears flicked with interest. I hoped Kirsty had been right in saying that the boys always behaved well when they knew there were horses in the vicinity. Horses shy readily at unexpected and loud noises and though I was well insured in case of accident that kind of trouble could do no good at all to the reputation of the riding school.

When I arrived back at the stables I saw that Kirsty had returned and was in one of the loose boxes grooming her own particular favourite, the chestnut mare Gypsy. She looked less tired and smiled when I enquired if she was all right now.

'Yes, I'm fine, thanks. I'm sorry about this morning. I suppose I was a bit over enthusiastic.'

'Never mind. Just take it a bit easier next time. I need my helpers on two feet.' She turned back to the grooming and I hesitated before saying: 'Your brother was here earlier.'

'Oh!' Her eyes were troubled as she turned back to me, and I had no need to tell her why her brother had come to see me. She chewed uneasily on her lower lip and said: 'He thinks he knows what's best for me. He doesn't see that I need to do something on my own. I guessed he might come but I hoped you would be able to persuade him to let me work here.'

I almost told her why it was unlikely that I could ever persuade her brother about anything, but the incident was not at all kind to me so in a cowardly fashion I forebore to mention it. 'You have to decide for yourself, Kirsty. Don't let him bully you into leaving if you don't want to. But if you get tired you must rest. This morning I didn't realize that I was letting you overdo it. On other days, when Diane is here, there's no need for you to over-tire yourself. Perhaps we could shorten your hours a little.'

I repeated this again on Saturday. I had told her she wasn't to work at the weekends but she insisted on coming in for the first two or three Saturdays when I would certainly need extra help in organization. This was the first day of full rides with hacks and lessons. The schedule was tight and I had more or less followed the existing pattern which meant that lessons began at nine and continued through until the afternoon hack, with a one and a half hour break at lunch time. We were by no means fully booked though Kirsty told me there were more clients than usual; probably they had come out of curiosity. But the pick of the animals were in use and on the whole I was satisfied with the way things went. I decided that a few advertisements in the local papers might not come amiss and perhaps I might try something like private lessons later on, particularly during the week. Janine had had several private pupils at her riding school, I remembered, and through the summer had taken jumping courses at all levels. There were plenty of things that could be done to improve the image of a riding school and make the place more attractive to potential customers. All that was required was a little imagination and I didn't think I lacked that.

I organized the day so that I took the more advanced riders in the big school. An artificial fibrous surface was due to be laid during the following week but fortunately it hadn't rained for a fortnight so the existing surface was at least workable.

Kirsty was looking tired so I sent her into the cottage to sit down. Diane and Jenny had been working very hard all day with the beginners so I said I would take out the final hack.

'You won't know the way,' Diane

objected. 'I usually take the Saturday afternoon country ride.'

'Jenny is coming with me today. I'd rather you stayed and organized the evening feeds.'

She jutted her chin and momentarily stared fiercely at me but I returned the glare and eventually it was she who gave in, nodding brusquely and walking away from me.

As it turned out, I was more than glad that I hadn't given in but went on the ride. It was a shambles — long string of ponies spread out far too much, many of the riders in the rear not really up to such a long ride. We cantered along a broad grassy track with me in the lead on Lady and Jenny in the rear on 'escort' duty. She had assured me that everyone was up to cantering and of course they were all equipped with hard hats, but when I glanced back it looked as though they were practising for the Grand National with seven or eight ponies spread over the track and little girls clinging on for dear life. It was a ridiculous situation, asking for accidents, and just one more thing to be sorted out. Perhaps it would be possible to organize two different country rides, one for more experienced riders, one for virtual beginners.

★ ★ ★

During the next few weeks I found plenty of things that needed sorting out, but by not doing too much, by concentrating on the really important jobs first, things gradually did get done. The important matters involved getting the graded training scheme going for the girls, having the schooling area drained and covered with the artificial surface; the cottage had to be made habitable and the yard was cleared up, the muddy surface covered by a thick layer of hard pressed gravel and all the woodwork painted. It was hard work and I couldn't have said at the time whether or not I was actually enjoying it. I fell into bed each night, asleep almost before I had pulled the duvet over me. My private life was nil but I had no time to regret that; which was probably just as well or I might otherwise have begun to miss Martin and the varied social life I had enjoyed at home. On one or two occasions when I did have a moment to think — usually when I was soaking in a bath — I would look at my work roughened hands and think of how disparaging I had been about the appearance of Julia Symonds. It had been all too easy to let myself go — my hair, which had always been shampooed and blow dried at least twice a week, had to make do with a quick wash once a week; my nails, always long, beautifully manicured, covered in a glossy coat of varnish, I had cut short soon after the first two broke off. I had brought with me to Hillcroft quite a varied wardrobe including a couple of very expensive model dresses but none of these had been worn. Instead I wore jeans or cords and shapeless jumpers. It didn't seem to matter; I could see that the school was looking better, more efficiently run, clean and less neglected, and there was no doubt that the number of customers had increased greatly. It was what I had wanted for a very long time and if I did sometimes yearn to dress up to the nines and go off somewhere special, the yearnings were swiftly gone and seldom repeated.

5

I had finally persuaded Kirsty that her health would hold out much better if she worked part-time so now she worked every afternoon and into the early evening. With Diane full-time and Jenny still coming in at the weekends, the work load was well spread out so that nearing the end of the summer term, with the prospect ahead of the school holidays, I felt that we were well able to cope. Working part-time seemed to suit Kirsty. I gathered that she had suffered from rheumatic fever as a child and had since tired very readily but now she looked suntanned, happy and healthy. Just a few days before the school holidays were due to begin, however, she did not turn up as usual at two o'clock.

It was fortunate that Jenny was in the yard, having been practising for a dressage competition she was entering, and she volunteered to take the afternoon country ride out. Diane had a private lesson in the school with three sisters whom she had always taught so I found myself with a bit of time to give Lady a much needed thorough grooming. She was enjoying life in the stables as much as I had hoped; most of the other horses were good natured creatures and in the field Lady had progressed naturally up the hierarchy that existed there until she was definitely queen of the roost, which suited her very well. I wasn't able to ride her as much as I would have liked as so much of my time was taken up with teaching, but Kirsty, with her naturally light hands and seat, could be trusted to ride her with perfect confidence.

It was very quiet in the yard. All the helpers were still at school of course and the week days were seldom busy. I slipped a halter on Lady and tied her head near the hay bale, then began the slow, rhythmic brushing that was always so soothing to me. Daddy, I remembered, thinking of my former life imperfectly, as though it were part of a film I had once seen, had never cared for this part of the business of riding. He had quite liked seeing me rigged out for a show in black coat, shining leather boots and spotless white jodhpurs; he kept all the press cuttings that mentioned me and was even heard to drop into a conversation the fact that I had won a prize or rosette at a show. But he had not approved the other side, the grooming, the tack cleaning, especially not the iniquitous 'mucking out'! He had wanted me to have a groom which of course was ridiculous for one horse. Besides, to me at the age of fourteen all this was part of the joy of having a horse of my own and I could never sacrifice any part of it. I still felt it was part of it. Anyone who knows anything about horses will agree that the way really to build up a relationship with a horse is to look after it in all ways.

So in the peaceful summer afternoon's silence I was brushing the mud
out of Lady's soft grey coat and
noticing the darker, almost dappled
patches coming out on her rump where
she was getting her smooth summer
coat, when I heard a car coming into
the yard. I briefly glanced up from my
task but when I saw the car I
straightened up completely and went to
look out over the stable door. It was a
massive Mercedes, dark blue in colour
and with the kind of sparkling surface
generally found only in cars that are
driven and cared for by a chauffeur.
And this one, I saw, did indeed have a
chauffeur, livery and all. He parked the
car in the yard and quickly got out in
order to go round and open the rear
door. The man who appeared was big
and, in his way, as gleaming and sleek
and expensive looking as the car.

It was all overdone just a little,
especially against the setting of the
yard, but not very obviously so. Perhaps
if I were not used to seeing Daddy and

Martin and some of Daddy's friends all dressed up, I might have thought this man extremely elegant and smart. As it was, I looked beyond the well cut Saville Row suit to the flashy diamond cuff links, the rock-like diamond on the second finger of one hand, the sovereign ring that adorned another finger, the gold identity bracelet against one snow white silk cuff. He looked worth a fortune and apparently carried a goodish part of that fortune around with him.

He was looking round in a frowning sort of way, so I called out: 'Can I help you?' and then he saw me and walked across the yard towards me.

'Who are you?' he demanded, in a rough voice that was accented but unrecognizably so. He was about fifty, handsome enough with thick dark hair and surprisingly blue eyes, but there was flabbiness about the jowls and the suit was stretched across his middle. I wondered if he had come to book lessons, which seemed most unlikely, but I could think of nothing else.

'I'm Lindsay Henderson, the owner of Hillcroft,' I explained, despite myself not able to keep a hint of pride from my voice.

'Oh, you are, are you? So it's true, what I heard, that the old goat has got out. How much did you pay for the place?'

I felt my mouth drop open in astonishment and my eyes widened. I now recognized that the accent was watered down Birmingham and at close quarters I read belligerance and unpleasantness in the small eyes and thrusting jaw.

'Whatever it was, I'll up it by ten thousand,' he continued before I could think how to reply.

'Really, Mr . . . '

'Lawson's the name. Matthew Lawson. You'll have heard of me, I daresay.'

'No, I don't think I have.' As I said this I felt that in fact the name had struck a chord in my memory, then I realized that Kirsty had mentioned him.

He was the man who believed that everything had its price.

Instinctively I knew it would be wise to treat this man with a certain amount of diplomacy so I bit down the curt, snapping remark I had been about to make on the lines of him minding his own business, and said carefully: 'I haven't been here long, Mr Lawson, and I certainly don't want to sell Hillcroft.'

In reply he glanced round the yard and finally brought his cold eyed stare back to Lady who had turned her head from the hay bale and seemed to be watching him interestedly.

'You've done a good bit to the place I can see, cleaned it up a bit, got some good horseflesh. I like to see private enterprise and the evidence of hard work. Well, I'm not one to quibble over details. I want this place for my girl. Set her heart on it she has and I've always made sure she gets whatever she sets her heart on. No messing now, Miss . . . er . . . Henderson. I'll up that offer to twenty thousand over whatever you paid for it. Now you can't complain about that, can you?'

I couldn't. I had been told that when my father wanted something badly enough he behaved like this. It was astonishing to meet such an attitude firsthand.

'Really, Mr Lawson, I told you I don't want to sell and I meant it.'

His jaw jutted and I felt rather than saw the big body stiffen beneath the expensive suit. 'I'll meet any price you care to make.'

'It isn't a matter of money!'

'Rubbish, girl. Everyone has their price.'

There, it was said, just as Kirsty had told me. I could hardly believe my ears. 'Not me. I have no intention of selling Hillcroft to anyone. And now, if you will excuse me, I am rather busy.'

Deliberately I turned away and began to rub the brush over Lady's gleaming sides with strokes that must have had more pressure than she was accustomed to for she moved restlessly away from me. I eased the pressure and felt her relax. I was listening for the sound of the Mercedes' engine starting up but it didn't come and I knew from the shadow across the wall of the loose box that Matthew Lawson still stood there. It was very difficult to stop myself turning round to look at him and took all my concentration to continue grooming Lady.

'I'll be back to make this offer again,' Lawson suddenly barked out, the words spoken in such a loud and gravelly voice that I jumped nervously and Lady copied my action. 'I don't give up easy, miss, as anyone who knows me will tell you.'

He strode off then, towards his car, and I stood by Lady watching over the top of the stable door. The chauffeur opened the door for him and in a moment had driven the big car out of the yard into the lane, passing as it did so Alan Wentworth's Range Rover. He was just what I needed then, I thought resignedly and contemplated ducking down in the hope that he hadn't seen me. He braked the vehicle in the gateway and I saw him wind down the window and glance back over his shoulder at the departing Mercedes, before driving further into the yard. I presumed he was here to see Diane and I quietly withdrew to Lady, brushing her in a half-hearted fashion as I thought again about Lawson and the comparisons I had drawn with my own father. Then once more I was aware of a shadow across the wall, also a big, broad shadow, and I waited for him to speak before looking round. Eventually, when he said nothing, I was forced to look round. He stood watching Lady and myself and I surprised a faintly brooding expression on the craggy face.

'Beautiful,' he remarked, in a soft voice.

I was startled. 'I beg your pardon!'

'The mare,' he explained with a little, tight smile. 'She's a beauty. Your own?'

'Of course.'

'Of course,' he repeated, sarcasm creeping into the deep voice. 'I don't suppose an ordinary riding school pony would be good enough for Miss Lindsay Henderson.'

I felt my face grow hot. I hadn't liked the way he spoke. It was almost as though he knew more about me than I cared for him, or indeed anyone round here in Wickham, to know.

'I've had Lady for several years, since she was a foal. Naturally I brought her with me.' I was angry then that I had seen the need to defend myself. 'Did you want something, Mr Wentworth? If you want to see Diane she's round in the school.'

'I don't. I came to tell you that Kirsty is unwell and won't be working for a few days.'

'Oh, dear. I'm sorry to hear that.'

'Are you?' he asked nastily. 'I don't see why you should be since you're the chief cause of this present bout of illness.' Before I could speak a word he went on, 'I warned you that she wasn't very strong but of course that cut no ice with you. People like you are only interested in themselves and everyone else can go to hell.'

On the whole I had always been quite good at rows, well able to hold my own without much trouble, but somehow every disagreement I had had with Alan Wentworth ended badly for me. Basically I was honest enough to admit to myself that this was because generally I was pretty much in the wrong. However, I swallowed hot words and tried to speak in a reasonable way.

'Kirsty has been working part-time only, as you know, and that was at my suggestion. She hasn't been overworked either. And despite what you think, I do care and I am sorry. I'll come and see her this evening.'

'Don't bother.'

'If I choose to bother, that's my affair and not yours!' I flashed out and there was a brief pause while we stared at one another and I wondered whether there would always be this antagonism between us and if there was anything I could do about it. Just as I was wondering with surprise why I should feel even the smallest desire to change it, Lady moved restlessly between us and he reached out an outstretched hand so that she nuzzled at his palm with her soft, silky nose.

'What did Matthew Lawson want?' he asked in a voice that was so carefully controlled and casual that there was no possible way I could fail to see the actual importance of the question.

'He was offering to buy the stables.'

'Oh, still at that old game, is he? He was forever offering Julia fantastic amounts of money, far more than the place is actually worth.' He looked consideringly at me, asking, as if he really wanted to know: 'Why didn't you accept? Think of the profit you'd have made in just a few weeks.'

'How do you know I didn't accept?'

'Did you?'

'As it happens, no. I have no intention of selling. Why should I?

Anyone would think you had a vested interest in getting me out.'

'Not at all,' he replied smoothly, sounding faintly amused. 'But this hasn't been a very lucky place. Julia had a string of misfortunes.'

There it was again; I was fed up to the teeth with hearing about Julia Symonds' misfortunes. 'Kirsty told me most of that bad luck was due to carelessness, that Miss Symonds just couldn't cope,' I said, and he shrugged.

'That may be so,' he admitted. 'Kirsty spends more time here than I do. But Julia cared very much for the stables. Sure things were pretty run down but she'd got tired and old beyond her years. She coped much better a few years back.' He regarded me steadily for a few moments, his eyes thoughtful though no longer antagonistic, and said, scathingly, 'You shouldn't talk so glibly about carelessness and coping. You're young and you seem to have plenty of energy and enthusiasm as well as an unlimited cash supply. Do you think, given Julia's circumstances, that *you* could cope?'

'I don't know,' I replied, angry at the smug way he said this, as though he would enjoy seeing me unable to cope 'but I do know this much, Mr Wentworth, if I ever find I can't cope, I'm damned if I'll ever sell Hillcroft to you. I think I'd rather sell to Matthew Lawson.'

The look he gave me then was neither surprised nor angry. In fact it was almost bleak. Then he simply turned his back on me and strode to the Range Rover, and I watched as he skilfully manoeuvred the vehicle at breakneck speed out of the yard. I watched his departure in bemusement, wondering if I had meant what I said. On the whole I thought not. For one thing, looking round the yard now, sparkling clean and bright in the sunlight, the few horses on view healthy and alert, the flowers bright in their whitewashed stone pots, the freshly laid gravel gleaming almost gold in the sun, it wasn't in me to admit that there could ever come a time when I couldn't cope.

★ ★ ★

I thought it diplomatic to phone the Wentworth home before going there, hoping to talk to Kirsty, but in fact the phone was answered by Mrs Parker, who was their housekeeper. I had met her a couple of times in the village, an elderly, very typical housekeeper type, fat and motherly, who had worked for the Wentworths when Alan's and Kirsty's grandparents were still alive. She spoke now with concern for Kirsty but I was pleased to realize that she, at least, didn't blame me for her illness.

'She's got a very nasty chest cold,' she explained, 'And as such things in her sometimes lead to bronchitis, Mr Wentworth thought it as well to get in the doctor. He said she was to have a few days indoors resting and mustn't overdo things for a week or two.'

'I see.'

For a moment I was struck by self-doubt. Had I been wrong, pig headedly determined that Alan Wentworth was fussing over nothing, that my reaching for freedom had to be mirrored by Kirsty's? 'I didn't realize she was that bad. Would it be all right if I came to see her now — can she see anyone?'

'Bless you, yes, my dear. At the moment it's only a cold. You come along whenever you like. I know she'll be pleased to see you.' The housekeeper chuckled. 'Real taken with you, she is. It's Lindsay this and Lindsay that.'

As flattering as this might be, I wished it were not so and fervently hoped Kirsty didn't mention my name too often in her brother's hearing. I replaced the receiver and went outside. A couple of older girls who went to the nearby comprehensive school had arrived and were grooming one of the ponies in the early evening sunshine. I called to them, telling them I would be back in an hour and walked out of the yard and down the lane, turning right towards the Wentworth property.

It was called, unimaginatively, Manor Farm, and I supposed the farm house, a large, grey stone building with an imposing façade and the remnants of what must have been a courtyard complete with fountain before it, had once been the local manor house. The farm buildings were at the rear of the house and out of sight. I had been here once, though never inside, and had heard local people talking about the farm and the way Alan ran it. He had been in the Royal Navy apparently, rising swiftly to the rank of First Lieutenant on a frigate, and his elder brother Ian was set to take over the farm. But in one incredibly tragic year for the Wentworths, both parents were killed in an air crash over Tenerife and not six months later Ian died when a piece of farm machinery fell and crushed his chest. Alan had come home almost at once, determined to provide a home for Kirsty, then twelve years old. Although he had never thought to take up farming as a career he had learned quickly and I knew that the farm was efficiently and economically run. This was a human and heart warming story but I refused to allow it to endear me to Alan Wentworth. He might be an excellent brother but as far as I was concerned, he was public enemy number one.

6

Kirsty listened with wide eyed interest as I recounted to her the visit of Matthew Lawson. I had found her up, sitting in front of a large fire in the living room of the beautiful old house. I realized I should have ascertained beforehand whether or not Alan was at home, but having neglected to do so, there wasn't much I could do when it was he who opened the door to me. He was very taciturn and forbidding but showed me into the room where Kirsty was and told me in a flat, cold voice not to stay too long, before closing the door firmly between us. Kirsty was wrapped comfortably in a woollen dressing gown; she had been reading a magazine but this she put down and smiled with real warmth at me; the large tabby cat on her lap blinked at me with lazy yellow eyes.

We went through the usual enquiries about her health. She was, she told me, perfectly all right, it was only a little chest cold and Alan and Mrs Parker were fussing over nothing. But as she spoke her breathing was ragged and spasmodic and she was very pale, but she seemed quite cheerful and when I told her about my visitor she clearly forgot all about her health.

'I went to school with Delia, his daughter,' she told me, somewhat breathlessly. 'I never realized he wanted the stables for *her*. Oh, how silly! As though she would ever be able to cope. She can't even ride very well. He used to spend fortunes on very expensive ponies for her and then wonder why she still couldn't win anything even at the local shows. She's a spoilt brat and it would be awful if she did have the stables. Apart from the fact that she'd certainly lose interest in no time, she was never very kind to the poor animals she did have. Often, if they refused a fence, always because of her poor riding, she would really lay into them.'

'Mr Lawson told me that he always gives his daughter what she wants.'

While we were talking, Alan came in and for a moment stood near the door listening. I was acutely aware of his silent presence and when I glanced surreptitiously in that direction saw that his eyes were on my face, which only served to increase my nervousness. I struggled to keep calm, annoyed with myself at being affected by him in this way. For a moment I paused to wonder what in the world had happened to the Lindsay Henderson of old. No man had ever made me blush and act like a tongue-tied schoolgirl as this man did, no man anyway except Martin and that, after all, had been a very different matter.

After a moment or two of this war of nerves — at least that was how I saw it — he crossed the room to a table where there was a tray with a decanter and glasses and he poured sherry into two of them, handing one to me without a word being spoken, and sipping the other himself. Presumably Kirsty's medication prevented her from taking alcohol. Then he moved to take up a typically male stance, legs apart before the empty fireplace. The conversation changed to how I would manage without Kirsty and I told her that of course we would manage and that she wasn't to worry. The atmosphere was reasonably friendly and suddenly I found myself asking:

'Do you know Matthew Lawson well, Mr Wentworth?'

Kirsty giggled. 'For goodness sake, Lindsay. No one ever calls him Mr Wentworth.'

We both ignored this, I with studied indifference, making it clear that I certainly had no intention of calling him Alan, and he as though he didn't care one way or another. He replied to my question slowly, as though he gave the subject some thought.

'I couldn't say I really know him. I

have met him socially a couple of times when Kirsty and his daughter were at St Agatha's together, but that's hardly knowing him.'

'What's he like?'

'Like?' Alan frowned. 'Tough — perhaps even ruthless — probably not a nice man to cross.'

'I thought that. Do you think he ever put any . . . well, any pressure on Miss Symonds to try to make her sell the stables to him?'

Our eyes met. His were startled and then wryly amused. 'Such as what?' he enquired. 'Manufacturing a run of bad luck so that the riding school would lose it's reputation and stop making a profit?'

Put like that the vivid idea that had come so suddenly into my mind sounded stupid and melodramatic. I coloured hotly, aware that he was finding my confusion highly amusing. 'It sounds ridiculous, put into words.'

'I don't know about ridiculous but highly improbable.'

'Nevertheless you wouldn't recommend that I should ever sell the stables to him.'

His eyes narrowed in that unnerving way I had noticed before as though he were determined I shouldn't know what he was thinking. Then he said, slowly and deliberately: 'Really, Miss Henderson, it strikes me you are far too efficient a young woman to think of giving up so easily. Besides, I thought the riding school was doing quite well.'

'It is. I thought you believed the reason to be other than my efficiency.'

A faint smile touched his mouth, softening its hard lines. I felt I had scored a hit, a very small one, but nevertheless a hit of sorts. He gave a little half shake of his head. 'Perhaps you misunderstand me.'

'I don't think so.'

Kirsty had been staring between us in puzzlement but I decided to leave it to Alan to explain if he so wished. I stood up quickly. 'I must be going. Thank you for the sherry. I'll call again, Kirsty.

Look after yourself and don't worry about coming back until you're really fit again.'

* * *

I walked quickly up the lane, my head lowered, still rather bemused by the conversation with Alan Wentworth. What, if anything, had it meant? It had seemed to me that more was left unsaid than had been said. But as I neared the stables something happened to take all this off my mind. I became aware of young female voices raised in — not cries exactly — but shouts of concern, and round the corner came a group of five young girls, each carrying a halter. A quick glance to the left showed me that all our ponies and the liveries were safely in the field on the hill, so what was all this?

Their faces were worried and Sally, the eldest, who was fourteen and had got through the first three grades of my new training scheme without much effort, came ahead, chewing miserably on her lower lip.

'Have you . . . you haven't seen Lady, have you?'

'Lady?' I have heard of people's blood running cold but until that moment I had never understood the full meaning of the phrase. I felt literally frozen by a numbing sensation that left me feeling sick.

'Of course I haven't seen Lady. What do you mean, Sally?'

'She got out — the loose box door was open — someone must have pushed the bolt across. We didn't see her go.'

'The door was shut,' little Janice Stafford insisted, coming up beside Sally. 'I'm sure it was. You were in there, weren't you, Lindsay, grooming her, and after, I went over and gave her an apple and . . . ' Her face puckered into near tears. 'They keep saying I must have pushed the bolt back but I never touched it.'

'I'm sure you didn't, Janice,' I

managed to say in a soothing manner I was far from feeling. I forced myself to sound casual as I took the halter from her.

'Where's Diane?'

'She's gone home.'

Home! Amazing how that girl was never around when I really wanted her. 'All right. Look, I'll go back down here towards the village. Janice, you come with me. Sally, you three go back the other way, towards the woods. That's the way we go for country rides so she may have headed in that direction.'

As I turned and hurried back the way I had come, Janice trotted beside me, again and again reiterating her belief that the stable door had been locked when she fed the apple to Lady. I saw no reason to believe she had unlocked the door and I was positive *I* had locked it. It was true that I couldn't actually remember the action — it was too much of an automatic thing to do — but I was sure I would never have left the bolt back.

I was thinking in a blurred and frightened way about runs of so-called bad luck, my thoughts in no way coherent, when Janice shouted, 'Oh, there she is!' with great relief in her voice, and before I could stop her she ran forward.

We had passed the fork in the lane which led to the Wentworth farm, which was why I had not seen Lady on my way back from there. She had been cropping grass in a fairly quiet way by a barbed wire fence that separated a field of wheat from the lane. I probably could have caught her without too much trouble but she had not run loose for some time now and was obviously in a state at finding herself suddenly free and in unknown territory. When Janice rushed at her, she lifted her head, snorted fearfully and trotted a little farther away, the early evening wind catching her tail and mane and lifting them into clouds of silver reflected by the sun. Any other time and I might have admired the attractive picture she made, but now my mouth was dry with fear for not much more than a mile away the lane opened out on to the busy dual carriageway that led to Salisbury.

'Wait, Janice,' I urged desperately. 'Look, I'll try to get round her and drive her back. When she sees the stables she'll probably go home. You wait here. On no account must we startle her.'

Janice nodded and obediently stood still while I quietly moved forward, keeping away from the mare, attempting to circle round to get in front of her, talking all the while in a soft and soothing voice; her ears flickered in recognition of my voice though she still moved her head nervously. I was just thinking that my strategy was going to work when from somewhere very close a motor bike engine revved up very loudly and savagely. I stood helpless with rage and fear as Lady lifted up her back legs, bucked high and galloped off towards the main road.

'Oh, God!' I whispered and, Janice at my heels, began to run after her. I didn't know what I could do. If Lady got on the main road with its four wide lanes and narrow central reservation there was almost certain to be an accident and I couldn't stand to think of the details of such an accident.

She had disappeared by the time I reached the next corner. I stood helpless, looking in all directions. Here the lane forked into two and it was possible that Lady may have gone down the narrowest way that led only to a farm. I could only hope so yet didn't dare hope.

'You go that way,' I told Janice, pointing down there. 'And I'll go towards the road. I don't know if . . . '

'Oh, look!' Janice cried, a little sob catching her voice. I followed the direction she was pointing and could very easily have cried myself.

Alan Wentworth had removed the leather belt from round his waist and had it looped round Lady's neck, an improvised halter that she was accepting with a meekness far more characteristic of her than had been her headlong flight. I managed somehow to approach at a walk though I longed to run. She had worked herself up into a sweat, her lovely grey coat glistened and was lathered along the flanks, and her sides heaved. There were tears in my eyes that I made no attempt to hide and though later I might have wished anyone in the world other than him to have been the one to have caught her, at that moment I could have hugged the big, broad body of Alan Wentworth. My defences towards him were utterly crushed and I didn't care a bit about trying to hide my relief or my gratitude.

'Oh, thank you, thank you,' I whispered, reaching up and running one hand down Lady's sweating neck. 'I thought she might have gone on the road. We had almost caught her and some idiot revved up a motor bike. I was imagining all kinds of things.'

'She almost did go on the road,' he

said shortly. 'Fortunately some sort of instinct turned her away and my men and I were able to catch her. God knows what kind of accident your carelessness might have caused.'

His disapproval and grimness got through to me, pushing away my relief and delight. I looked at him across Lady's withers, blinking hard to rid my eyes of the tears that were still there.

'Carelessness?' I managed to say. 'It wasn't . . . I shut the door. I don't know . . .'

'Another bit of bad luck?' he inquired with biting sarcasm. 'You'll be saying next that Matt Lawson was lurking somewhere, hiding in the barn maybe, ready to nip out when no one was looking and undo the stable door. Or maybe the mare reached over and undid the bolt herself. Do yourself a favour, Miss Henderson, and face the fact that this just isn't your life. All you've done is live up to the idea of you that I first had. Why the hell don't you just give up and go back to wherever you came from?'

I felt the colour drain out of my face and I took a step back as though to get away from the horrible words. I felt sick and was struck by the absurdest desire to cry. Instead I managed somehow to keep control of myself. I would have liked to find something equally as nasty to say to him but my mind was blank and hurt. It was probably as well. After all, he had taken the trouble to catch Lady and bring her straight back and the least I could do was to swallow my pride and repeat my first relieved thanks. I quickly slipped the halter over Lady's head and undid the belt that had held her, handing it back to him with hands that trembled slightly.

'I know that I locked the door to Lady's stable. How she got out I don't know, but I do know it wasn't through carelessness either of myself or the girls. Thank you for bringing her back, Mr Wentworth. I'm so sorry to have caused you so much trouble.'

It would have sounded very dignified

if my voice hadn't trembled so. I turned away then, pulling at the rope so that Lady followed me. I did not turn round at all until I had reached the end of the lane, then I risked a quick look back over my shoulder. But I needn't have bothered for Alan Wentworth had gone.

★　★　★

Until then I had been fortunate enough not to need to call in the vet, which was all to the good because as everyone knows, vets' fees are pretty heavy these days. It was altogether too expensive to insure all the horses against accident although Lady was insured as she always had been. The riding school animals were all fairly hardy and healthy but the day following Lady's escapade which left her none the worse for her experience, one of the ponies, a kind natured grey called Archie, went lame having got a stone in his hoof. I extricated the stone but his foot was badly bruised so I rang the vet whom

Miss Symonds had recommended, a Jack Blake, who lived in Wickham though he belonged to a group partnership in Andover. He came later that day driving into the yard in a dark green shooting brake.

He was younger than I had expected, perhaps in his mid thirties, tall and thin with sandy hair and friendly blue eyes behind steel rimmed spectacles. Having dealt with Archie's foot, he accepted my invitation to a cup of coffee.

'I was wondering if you'd decided to go to one of the other veterinary practices,' he told me, munching a digestive biscuit from the proferred tin. 'You've been here — how long?'

'Two months.'

'Two months, and you haven't had to call a vet?'

'There's been no necessity until now.'

'If everyone was like you, we'd be out of business.' He had picked up Tigger, one of the cats that came purring round his legs, and his hands stroked her with

130

expert ease. 'Hello, I detect a pregnancy.'

'I know,' I said ruefully. 'I suppose stables and cats go together but once she's had the kittens I think I'll have her spayed.'

'Good idea,' he agreed. 'So, you've had some good luck with the ponies' health.'

It was a nice change to hear Hillcroft connected with good luck, and I was tempted to say so to Jack Blake but my last encounter with Alan Wentworth still rankled and I was reluctant to have another man think me an over-imaginative scare-monger. So we talked about other things, about Lady's pedigree, about how the riding school was doing business-wise, about how I was settling in in Wickham. Jack told me that though he was fortunate to secure a place in his present partnership, he had never wanted to leave Wickham to live anywhere else. At this point he added:

'Obviously you haven't been out and

about much. I thought I might have seen you down at the White Horse maybe, or at the badminton club in the village hall.'

I smiled, briefly imagining my father's reaction to the idea of his daughter playing badminton in the village hall. My reasons, however, for not joining this or any other of many village activities, were more prosaic and far less snobbish.

'I've been too busy and by the end of the day I'm too whacked for anything, most of all for anything strenuous like badminton.'

'Sitting in a comfortable bar having a drink isn't a bit strenuous,' Jack insisted. 'I think you ought to get out a bit, get away from here. Being industrious is all very well but everyone needs some recreation. How about joining me for a drink tonight?'

Which was how it was that eight o'clock found me sitting in the chintzy lounge bar of the White Horse hotel, the only pub in Wickham. Jack was right. I did need to relax and I had been as pleased and as idiotically excited by his casual invitation as any young girl on her first date. For one thing, it offered me the much needed opportunity to get out of jeans and shirts and into some more feminine gear. I had never, unfortunately, frequented local pubs and had no idea how to dress. Equally, I realized I couldn't possibly admit to such an odd and curiosity-provoking fact to anyone in order to seek advice. So I put on a long sleeved silk blouse and a grey pleated skirt which clothes I realized at once were perfectly all right. I applied make-up for the first time in months and actually blow dried my hair instead of letting it dry naturally. This action made me realize that it was long and rather straggly and badly in need of a re-shape, but at least it was still glossy and in good condition. I didn't reckon I looked too bad — not a patch on my former glamorous self but well enough to earn a look of admiration from Jack.

When asked, I said I would have a lager. This was by no means my usual drink but it was so long since I had touched alcohol other than the small sherry Alan Wentworth gave me, that I didn't trust my head with a gin and tonic.

While we were sitting on high stools at the bar, several people talked to Jack and he introduced them all to me. I realized how isolated I had been for I knew none of these locals though they seemed to know all about me and about the riding school.

'I saw that grey mare of yours tear off past our back garden,' one man told me. 'Proper took me back it did to when Julia Symonds' horses were forever getting out and traipsing all over people's gardens.'

'Did that happen often?' I enquired innocently. 'I did hear of one occasion when a pony had to be put down.'

'Oh, yes, that was nasty, poor beast. But usually they got out by jumping the fence, maybe just two or three at a time.'

'The gate had been left open, the time Romany got out,' Jack put in. 'I remember the occasion well. I hadn't been in practice here more than a couple of weeks. I had been working in London and was still finding it a bit strange dealing with horses and cattle after handling nothing larger than dogs and cats.'

The conversation changed to different topics but I was thoughtful about what I had heard. It bore out what Kirsty had said. In fact the instances of horses getting out of their fields were rather more frequent than even she had implied and very possibly carelessness had indeed led to Julia Symonds' 'bad luck'.

As he returned from the bar with our second drinks, Jack's name was called from the public bar which was roughly at right angles to the lounge, with the two rooms making an L shape, the bar being at the junction. He answered and talked through to someone for a moment before returning to me.

'Would you like to go through to the public bar? It's a bit quiet in here and at least in there you'll have the chance to meet some more locals — we could have a game of darts. Ever played?'

'No.'

I didn't know what tone was in the monosyllable but he briefly frowned. I thought I had rid myself of that nasty streak of Henderson arrogance and was so startled at finding it still there, along with an even nastier bit of snobbery about public bars, that I blushed hotly. I managed a quick smile and knew from the way he immediately smiled back, that I had successfully quelled any doubts he may have had. 'I haven't the faintest idea how to play darts,' I told him.

'There's no time like the present to learn. Come on.'

The public bar was larger than the lounge, much busier and noisier and filled with a faint haze of cigarette smoke that was not being dealt with by the extractor fan that whirled noisily on one window. There was a bar billiards table with a group of laughing young men gathered round it and at a table in the corner four old men sat playing cards. Most of the other tables had people sitting round them and at the dart board were four people playing darts. The first person I recognized was Diane Fairburn. Then the man who was throwing darts turned and I saw that it was Alan Wentworth. Not the most propitious place to meet after our last encounter but I realized it was too late to back off now.

I followed Jack across the room, hearing him call: 'Mind if we join you? I'll chalk for this game.' He turned and introduced me, saying, 'Of course you'll know Alan and Diane, Lindsay. And probably Ted and Jean, too.' I knew Jean who brought her two girls riding every Saturday morning. Everyone smiled and nodded but I thought Diane's eyes were hard and she looked less than pleased to see me, though probably no more disconcerted to see me than I was to see her. Alan gave me a small though not unfriendly smile that did not reach his eyes and I purposely kept my greeting as coolly polite as his had been.

While they played darts and Jack marked up the scores on the blackboard, I watched and tried to make some sense of what was going on. They played three games, of which Alan and Diane won the first and last, which meant, apparently, that they would then play us.

'I don't suppose *you* know how to play darts,' Diane said in a spiteful way that seemed uncalled for. I decided it was not worth the effort of bluffing it out and probably making a bigger fool of myself than otherwise, and cheerfully replied:

'You suppose right. I've never thrown a dart in my life.'

'Everyone stand well clear,' Jack said and we all laughed, but very much to my surprise it was Alan who came and stood beside me and quickly and succinctly explained such intricacies as doubles and trebles and how the scoring went. When explained like this it seemed very clear and I thanked him warmly. At this he seemed to remember suddenly who I was and returned to the table where his beer was, stiff-faced.

I was allowed to throw a few darts to get some idea of what it felt like and to my surprise found it quite easy.

'You were having us on, you've played before,' Jack said a little later, when he and I beat Alan and Diane without much difficulty. Admittedly he had got all the important doubles but I hadn't found it very hard to hit the twenty section with most of my darts so our totals were high.

'Beginners' luck,' I said with a smile.

The evening progressed well with everyone apparently enjoying themselves, though I was sure Diane resented my presence. There seemed no reason for this and I thought I may have been imagining it, for she laughed and smiled and didn't seem to object when someone, Alan I think it was, suggested that she and I play the two men. We lost, though not very badly and then somehow, and I wasn't sure how, it transpired that in the next game I had Alan as my partner. Remembering that most of our past meetings had been far from friendly, I was amazed at how well we played together and how, when we were talking between games, there was none of our previous antagonism. Of course the genial, smoke filled pub atmosphere had a lot to do with this. It was what I supposed to be a typical, friendly Friday evening and no one had time for their normal, everyday dislikes. Nevertheless I was surprised at how happy and content I felt. Later, near the end of the evening, when we all left the dart board and the four of us sat round a small table and Jack and Alan grew temporarily serious as they discussed a rather unpleasant bit of news that Foot and Mouth disease was suspected on the Continent, I looked at Alan and wondered how it was that my own dislike had subtly changed during the evening to . . . what? Liking? Respect? I wasn't sure.

Then he happened to glance my way and for a brief moment our eyes met in that rather unnerving way that happens sometimes between people who are really little more than strangers, and I felt my face grow hot as I hastily looked away. I was more than relieved that the landlord chose that moment to ring the bell indicating that closing time was drawing near. Jack immediately drained his glass and stood up.

'Time to go. It's your busiest day tomorrow, Lindsay. Come on. I'll walk you home.'

We said goodnight to Alan and Diane and left them still sitting there. The moment we stood up Diane turned away and began talking to Alan in a quiet, intimate way, as though we had never been there. I glanced back before going through the door. Alan was in the process of draining the remaining beer from his glass, his eyes watching me over the rim.

The cold night air cooled my suddenly hot face. I didn't want to talk but to think, and Jack said something that made me want to think even more. He laughed softly as we began to walk up the road. He had his hands thrust deep into his trouser pockets and I was relieved by this indication that he had no romantic thoughts in mind. I didn't think I was capable of dealing with that.

'What's so funny?' I asked.

'Oh . . . I was just thinking about poor old Diane. She never gives up trying.'

'Trying?' I queried, though half guessing his meaning.

'Yes, trying to hook Alan. She's been trying her darnedest to get him to the altar since he left the Navy and came home to run the farm.'

'He presumably likes her well enough,' I said slowly. 'You'd think after all that time . . . '

'Well, I've always presumed she'd succeed eventually. Though of course there's Kirsty; she and Diane don't get on too well and Alan might be influenced by that. He's always looked after Kirsty and with her being so sickly there's a special relationship between them.'

As he went on telling me all about just how ill Kirsty had been in the past, how every winter she suffered badly from severe chest colds and occasionally bronchitis, I began to feel more and more that I had been wrong in my dealings with her brother, over her health. His protectiveness had been perfectly natural and in no way to be compared with the way my father had dominated my life. I suppose it proved how much the weeks at Hillcroft had changed me that I made a vow to apoligize as soon as I got the opportunity to do so.

Jack was speaking again, something more about Diane and Alan. I listened without much comprehension, having missed what went before.

' . . . of course whether Alan would use Kirsty's dislike of Diane as an excuse I don't know.'

'Surely if a man really wanted to marry a girl he wouldn't allow himself to be influenced by his sister.'

'I don't know. I guess Diane might have worn him down in the end, especially when there was no other girl on the scene. But things look a bit different now, don't they?'

'Do they?' I asked vaguely, not having the faintest idea what he was talking about.

'Don't you think so?' He gave me a wide, knowing grin.

'I have no idea,' I said quickly, and he laughed. As by then we had reached the cottage door, the conversation lapsed, for which I was more than glad, because despite my apparent vagueness I had known what Jack meant, or at least I thought I did. He had meant things were different now because of *me*; he thought Diane's unpleasantness towards me was because she was jealous. It was all nonsense of course, but very disturbing nonsense, the kind of nonsense that begins to plant seeds in a person's mind if they're not careful.

The cottage had never seemed so quiet or so lonely. I felt restless and disturbed and wished I had not gone out that evening. At the same time I knew that I would not have changed what had happened. Yet nothing had happened! It was all in Jack's imagination and in the way I interpreted his peculiar thoughts. It was because nothing had happened, yet I felt so strongly that something *had* happened, that I was so disturbed. And if that sounds cockeyed, it was no wonder I was so upset.

I made myself a hot drink and sat drinking it on the side of my bed. Then on impulse I got up and dug out my photograph album from the bedside cabinet. It was the one real reminder of my old life I had brought with me and I admit this was not the first time I had sat here brooding over it; in the early days of my life here I had often sat gloomily staring at the pictures of my father's house, of myself and Lady both immaculately turned out for a show, of myself at the wheel of Daddy's Rolls Royce, of Martin and me at a friend's garden party. Everytime I looked at them I had experienced a certain amount of doubt, regret and uncertainty. That was why over the last few weeks I had resisted the temptation to look at them. Now I turned the pages with exaggerated care and looked at each photograph in detail. But this time was different. I felt nothing, no regret, no nostalgia. It was like looking at pictures of complete strangers. Even Martin's handsome, dashing figure seemed far away and distant.

I went to bed more disturbed than before I had looked at the album and before I realized what was happening I had begun to cry. It didn't last long and I had no idea why I was crying, but the next morning I fully convinced myself that it must have been those last two gin and tonics that brought on the unaccustomed attack of the blues. Yet in my heart I knew this was untrue.

7

There was a small and fairly exclusive girls' prep school less than half a mile from Hillcroft and three times a week some of the pupils came for lessons or hacks. They were accompanied by a rather pleasant teacher named Miss Usher who usually stayed with me while I taught and willingly helped with such things as rearranging jumps, tightening girths, adjusting stirrup leathers and so on. The Tuesday afternoon following my evening out with Jack, it was a different mistress who came, a thin faced, miserable looking woman wearing jodhpurs and hacking jacket, who said she would go on the hack. She explained that she was the deputy headmistress, Miss Allayne and that she had come because she felt it was time the safety aspect of the riding school was looked into. I frowned at this.

'Have you had any complaints about safety? I can assure you no child is permitted to go on a country ride until she can adequately cope with the trot and canter in the school.'

'That is as maybe,' she replied in a snooty sort of voice. 'But I wish to look for myself. The parents pay a good deal of money towards these recreational activities and naturally we must be sure that they receive the best there is.'

'Naturally,' I echoed flatly.

'You have a mount for me? I will ride that pretty grey mare if she is free.' She had indicated Lady with an imperious nod of her head that really got my back up.

'She isn't, I'm afraid,' I said as pleasantly as possible, which I didn't think was actually very pleasant at all. 'Lady is my own mare.'

'I can assure you I am a very competent rider.'

'I daresay, but I'm afraid I can't let you ride Lady. I'll have one of the other horses saddled for you.'

She glared but said nothing more and I went away to find her a mount. Diane was mucking out one of the stables and I called to her:

'Tack up Patrick for me, Diane, please. Miss Allayne wants to join the hack.'

Diane merely nodded and went off to the tack room for Patrick's saddle and bridle. Her silence meant nothing. Since Friday evening we had scarcely exchanged half a dozen words. I walked over to the school where the girls were waiting for their lesson, passing Kirsty who was getting the other girls sorted out for the hack, and Miss Allayne who stood there impatiently waiting for her mount.

'Diane is just tacking up Patrick,' I told her as I walked past. 'She won't be a moment.'

I knew at once that my attitude towards the teacher was silly and unbusinesslike, deliberately getting her back up as it did. The business that came in from St Agatha's was important for the only other riders who came during the week in term times were a few housewives, or shift workers, and every penny counted. I did wonder as I began the lesson who had suggested that our hacks might be unsafe, for Miss Usher had always commented upon how careful we were. As it was, probably nothing more would have happened had the hack gone its normal way. Unfortunately, it didn't. I had finished the second of the two half hour lessons and was supervising the girls unsaddling their mounts and turning them into the meadows when the riders returned. At once I could tell that something was wrong. Kirsty in the lead was white faced and distressed. Most of the girls wore the looks of ill-suppressed excitement that youngsters often have when something unexpected happens to brighten up their lives. I also saw, to my astonishment, that Miss Allayne was mounted, not on Patrick, who was a lively bay gelding, but on Dillon, a dear old pony, fourteen years old and generally used for beginners only. Before I could think of turning and demanding of Diane what in the world she thought she was doing putting the woman on Dillon, I saw that Kirsty was leading Trusty, a normally quiet chestnut, whose neck and sides were flecked with sweat; the girl on Trusty's back had a face that was puffy and dirt streaked from crying.

'Oh, God!' I muttered. 'Now what?'

I went to Kirsty, anxious to hear from her before Miss Allayne got in on the act. 'It's all right,' she said hastily, her voice shaking. 'Honestly, no one's hurt. The child fell quite softly. It was on the grass track up beyond the farm. Trusty bolted down the track and then came to a dead halt where it turns sharply at the bend. I saw it all and I know she wasn't hurt, but — '

She got no further because by then Miss Allayne had dismounted and was storming at me. I didn't take much of it in, just the words 'irresponsible', 'badly trained animals', 'putting children on ponies far too strong for them'. I also gathered that part of her grievance was because she had been humiliated by having to ride old Dillon. The girl, a nasty, spoiled little brat if ever I saw one, began to cry again, though when I questioned her it was obvious that Kirsty was right, she was shaken but unhurt.

'Why did Trusty bolt?' I demanded, jumping in when Miss Allayne drew breath.

'He bolted because he is badly trained and — '

'That's nonsense!' I snapped. 'Trusty is normally quiet — something must have happened to cause him to bolt.'

'I was right beside the animal and I heard and saw nothing.'

I was silent a moment, looking at the ring of faces, but no one said anything more. Somehow I buried my pride enough to apologize and after a few more words of a similar sort from Miss Allayne, they all filed off to their coach.

As they did so, one of the girls came hurrying back, speaking in a low voice.

'Lindsay, I know what it was made Trusty bolt. It was the motor bike.'

'What motor bike? No one else mentioned a motor bike.'

'There was one though. I was at the back of the ride and I saw it. It was inside the field, behind the hedge, and just as Trusty went by the boy started up the engine.'

'But why didn't Miss Allayne hear it?'

The girl was silent a moment and glanced round hurriedly. 'I think she did,' she muttered, turning to rush to the coach. 'But she was just too angry to say so.'

'Out of the mouths of babes,' I muttered to myself. Diane was just going by and I called her. She had watched Miss Allayne giving me what-for with scarcely concealed delight and I was just about boiling over.

'I told you to put Miss Allayne on Patrick, not Dillon. What in the world possessed you to put her on him? You might have known any adult who can ride well would be annoyed at having to ride him.'

She opened her eyes very wide and innocently. 'Did you say Patrick? Gosh, I'm sorry. I could have sworn you said Dillon.'

I knew she was lying but there was nothing I could do about it, though I could cheerfully have stamped on her feet, or slapped a hand across her smiling mouth. Such primitive thoughts shocked me. I hadn't used to be so physical.

'Just listen a bit harder in future,' I told her, and went to the tack room where Kirsty was making coffee. When I had calmed down a bit I told her what the schoolgirl had said about the motor bike.

'Could it be true?' I asked her. She had regained a little of her colour now, thank goodness, and looked less shaken. It was sickening that this should happen on her first day back to work after her illness. I found myself wondering wryly what Alan would have to say about it. Would he blame *me*? More than likely.

Kirsty shrugged her narrow shoulders. 'I suppose so. If so, I wouldn't have heard anything, being up at the front. But I'd have thought other people would have — that Miss Allayne was right next to the girl on Trusty.'

I thought of what the other girl had said. 'If she had, she wouldn't have mentioned it. She was out to make trouble — she was already furious because I wouldn't let her ride Lady, and then Diane went and put her on Dillon. This happening just helped her to have something real to moan about.'

'I'm sorry, Lindsay.'

'Goodness, love, it's not your fault. The stupid old bat would have found something to moan about anyway. But what was a motor bike rider doing, deliberately frightening a pony like that? I'm just about fed up with these motor bikes. It was a bike engine that nearly sent Lady on to the main road last week.'

'I can't understand it,' Kirsty said, frowning. 'I know the lads practice their speedway riding up in the woods, they have done for a couple of years, but there's never been any trouble. They're always really good about being careful not to startle the horses. After all, some of them have sisters who ride here — Diane's youngest brother is one of them and he used to help down here.'

I finished my coffee and stood up. 'Tell you what, Kirsty, I'm going to ride up there and have a look round. I'd like to look for some evidence of a motor bike being up there, just in case the headmistress of St Agatha's rings up to complain. At least then I can say it wasn't anything we could help.'

'It would have to be Ursula Hargreaves who fell off. Most of the others would have taken it much better, but she's a beastly spoilt brat. Her father is terribly rich and dotes on her.' Kirsty heaved a sigh and got up, pushing the cat off her lap. 'God preserve me from the children of rich men,' she muttered.

I almost laughed aloud at the irony of this comment, though she was right. I was beginning to have a thing against rich men's daughters myself!

I rode Lady up to where Kirsty said Trusty had begun to bolt and hunted about in the undergrowth like an amateur detective, but the last few weeks had been very dry and the ground was hard. Certainly I found the grass flattened in places but that might have been caused by nothing more than a courting couple. Giving up the search despondently, I led Lady back to the path.

As we reached it she put up her head and whinnied softly. We were being watched by two pairs of curious eyes; one pair belonged to a very handsome bay gelding who stood on the other side of the track, the other pair were blue, faintly amused and belonged to Alan Wentworth. I would have liked very much to mount and leave quickly, for no one really cares to be caught out doing odd things such as searching along the hedgerow. However, he was too close for me merely to nod and ride away; also I remembered, in surprise, that our last meeting had actually been friendly.

'Found anything?' he asked, urging the bay forward.

'How did you . . . ?'

'Kirsty came out of the stables as I rode by and told me about the trouble.'

'I see. Do you think I'm being over dramatic?'

'I don't know. I've never heard of any of the local kids causing trouble with their bikes.'

'So I believe, but that child was convinced a motor bike engine had startled Trusty. Everyone keeps telling me the boys behave themselves but that's twice that one has almost caused an accident by revving up suddenly.'

'Oh? When was the other time?'

Reluctantly I told him. 'The day Lady got out. I had almost caught her when a motor bike revved up nearby and she bolted.'

'Did you see the bike?'

'No. It was behind a hedge. But I didn't imagine it.'

Unexpectedly he smiled. 'No, I don't think you did. But you don't seriously imagine Matthew Lawson is paying some kid to frighten your horses?'

'Of course I don't!'

'Then what on earth . . . '

What he intended saying I don't know for at that moment, from farther up the track, where it wound into the first bit of woodland, there came the sound of a motor bike engine starting up. We both stared in that direction then Alan actually laughed. 'The phantom motor bike rider rides again,' he said mockingly, and turned his horse's head in that direction.

'Where are you going?' I yelled, scrambling on to Lady's back.

The ground was quite soft here. Already his horse was cantering. I noticed how well he sat in the saddle, easy and relaxed and balanced, a natural horseman. The bay was big, probably seventeen hands, and Lady had to canter fast to keep up. Alan glanced once over his shoulder.

'Let's take a look,' he called, sounding as though he were enjoying himself.

'But you'll never catch a motor bike on horseback!'

'You want to bet?' he laughed.

We hurtled down the rutted grassy track and in amongst the trees. Alan obviously knew this area far better than I did and I was content to stay behind. I thought he was mad though it was ages sincc I had enjoyed quite such a reckless ride and I could tell by the way her ears twitched that Lady was loving it. Soon I realized that Alan wasn't mad at all. The track was certainly passable by motor bike but there was no way a bike, no matter how skilled the rider might be, could travel along here as swiftly as a horse could. We came to where the lane forked and I recognized the path then. It went on for about a mile before turning in a flattened circle, eventually coming back to the fork, and as far as I remembered there were no paths off. The trees here were mainly beech and hazel with the occasional clump of sweet chestnut, all growing very close together. There was no way our motor bike rider could branch off. Still laughing, Alan yelled back at me:

'You go to the right. I'll meet you at the top.'

We charged at a near gallop around the first bend and almost at once I glimpsed the vehicle ahead. It was actually only a scooter, which was no doubt why we were able to catch up so easily. The rider had been moving quite slowly but then he glanced back, saw me and increased his speed. The excitement of the chase gripped me then. Despite all the opportunities I had had all my life, I had never cared for fox hunting which seemed to have the odds altogether too heavily stacked on one side. But this was something else. I might feel a little ashamed later of these primitive instincts but at the time, with the adrenalin flowing and Lady's mane flapping in my face as I bent low over her neck to avoid the low sweeping branches, I felt more alive than I had ever felt.

We were perhaps forty or so feet behind when the lane curved sharply and for a moment scooter and rider were lost to my view. I remembered myself sufficiently to steady Lady as we took the corner and it was as well that I did for just in front of us was the scooter lying on its side, its rider in the process of scrambling out of the grass, and Alan steadying the bay, that was dancing about excitedly, before jumping to the ground. I wondered fleetingly if there would be a fight and with my excitement plummeting swiftly, fervently hoped not. When I saw the boy and Alan side by side I realized the idea was ludicrous. Alan, over six feet in height and big with it, could have flattened the boy with one hand.

I patted Lady's heaving neck and slid to the ground. Alan was saying, in a deep voice touched with disbelief, 'Colin Fairburn! What the hell are you doing?'

'I wasn't doing nothing!' the boy yelled back. His voice was very young and he sounded near to tears. When he took off his crash helmet, revealing his face more clearly, I saw that he couldn't have been more than about seventeen. He was young, a bit stupid looking, suffering from acne and altogether not a very prepossessing character. His name alone linked him with Diane.

'Why did you run away then?'

'I didn't! How would you like it if someone came charging after you on a bloody great horse, like she did?' He turned reproachful eyes on me and sniffed. I expected any minute that he would wipe his nose on his sleeve but thankfully he seemed content merely to sniff.

'Was it you who frightened Miss Henderson's horses?' Alan asked, still in the same good-humoured way. It seemed to me that he was treating this as a game and it annoyed me, though later I realized that angry words and threats would not have gained the results that his good-humoured voice did.

'You've worked in the stables. You must know running a motor right near the horses would frighten them.'

The boy shuffled his feet. 'I didn't do nothing. There's lots of us kids ride our bikes up here.'

'You were seen,' Alan said, the lie so glib that I almost believed it myself. Clearly poor Colin Fairburn — and incredibly I *was* thinking of him as 'poor' — believed him.

'I didn't mean no harm.'

'And fortunately none was done. What made you do it? You used to help round the stables. I thought you liked the place.'

Again sullen, watery eyes were turned on me. 'That was when Miss Symonds was there. She was okay. I liked her. But not this one. She's snooty and uppity.'

Since I had never set eyes on the boy before, nor presumably he on me, I opened my mouth to protest but Alan, catching my eye, frowned and shook his head. 'What makes you think that? You don't know Miss Henderson, do you?'

He shook his head. 'It's what our Di says. She's always telling me how she puts her down. Thinks she's better'n any one else an' all. I just thought it would be a bit of fun. It made Di laugh when I told her how the other one, the grey one, ran away. Gave me a quid, she did.'

This time I felt that I couldn't keep quiet. A muffled, strangled gasp of indignation escaped me in the face of this enormity and I was ready to say more. However, again Alan glanced at me and shook his head and again I somehow managed to keep quiet. Alan caught hold of the scooter and pulled it upright, saying as he did so: 'All right, you young idiot. Get out of it. And if I hear of any of the horses being frightened again I'll personally clip you round the ear. Go on, hop it!'

'Well, of all things!' I exploded, a moment later. 'How you could let him get away with it, after admitting . . . '

'Cool down, Lindsay,' he said, still using the same humouring tone he had used on Colin Fairburn. 'Couldn't you see he's a bit simple?'

'That isn't the point.'

'It is the point. He's not a bad kid. He used to help Julia a lot about the stables. He's easily influenced.'

'Yes, by Diane . . . and just wait till I get back to Hillcroft. I'll — '

'You'll calm down, for one thing.'

I had been about to turn and mount but now he took hold of my right arm as I reached up to the saddle. His fingers closed firmly, gently but with muscular inflexibility round my wrist. I stared at him, surprised and a little apprehensive. 'It won't do any good storming back and yelling at Diane.'

'Won't it? It'll do *me* a heck of a lot

167

of good. Give me one good reason why I shouldn't.'

He was silent a moment, looking down at me, and I felt the thumb of the hand that was holding mine moving against the inside of my wrist in a caressing gesture that was as intimate as it was disturbing. My temper, despite efforts to keep it up, began to die.

'I'm not trying to protect Diane,' he said.

'Aren't you?'

'No. She had no right to encourage Colin to do what he did. But you might try to think why she did it and try to understand a little.'

'Why should I always be trying to understand people? No one ever does much to understand my position.'

He smiled, softly, a little reflectively. 'Perhaps you don't need it. You are a remarkably well-adjusted person, Lindsay.'

'Oh, sure,' I said bitterly. 'Hard as nails, that's what you called me, isn't it? I'm supposed not to mind if people try

168

to ruin my business by frightening my horses so that people get thrown and for all I know putting people on unsuitable horses and leaving gates open.'

Obviously he didn't entirely understand this bit of gibberish for a quick frown creased between his eyes. I wished he would let go of me for the touch of his hand was so off putting, particularly now that he had transferred his grip from my wrist to my hand itself.

'Did I say you were hard as nails?' he smiled. 'Perhaps I was wrong about that. But you do seem to be pretty self-sufficient and that young Colin Fairburn is not. Neither is Diane for all the appearance of it.'

'Of course you would stick up for her!'

'Not for the reason you think. Look, she worked for Julia from the time she left school. She had been riding at Hillcroft since she was five and was over the moon when Julia offered her the job. She had a sort of hero worship of Julia and it came as a great shock to her when Julia announced that she was going to sell up and get out. She refused to notice how Julia had let Hillcroft run down and it's particularly galling to her that you are making such a success of it. It wouldn't have been so bad if someone like Julia had bought the place, but no, along came Miss Lindsay Henderson, beautiful, well-spoken, well-educated and sophisticated — in fact all the things Diane would love to be but never could be.'

I stared at him, my eyes wide. I hadn't, over the past weeks, got the impression that Alan saw me in those particular lights. I certainly didn't see myself like that, not any more.

'Are you suggesting I should just ignore what's happened?' I asked in a low voice.

'Not ignore it, but . . . is Diane a good worker? Julia always said she was.'

'Yes,' I admitted with extreme reluctance. 'She does work very hard.'

'I'm asking if you'll let me talk to her first.'

'Oh, for heaven's sake! I must be out of my mind!'

He laughed and released my hand. Without the contact I felt absurdly lost. 'Maybe, but will you?'

'I'll try to keep my mouth shut just for now, though it'll probably choke me.'

'Good girl. Thanks.' He gave me a leg up and put my left foot into its stirrup iron, neither of which action was entirely necessary but somehow rather pleasant for all that, and stood a moment, his hand over both mine as they rested on the pommel. I thought he was going to say something more, something of great importance; it seemed as though he were thinking about it. Then he shook his head very slightly as though he had changed his mind. He stepped back, gave Lady a goodnatured slap on the rump and said: 'See you later.' Quickly I pushed Lady into a trot and though I longed to look back, I kept my eyes fixed firmly on the track ahead.

★ ★ ★

Whether or not I would have been able to face Diane without saying something, I don't know, but my forebearance wasn't put to the test for on reaching the stables I was told by Kirsty that Diane had gone home.

'She had a headache and as there wasn't much else to do I suggested she went home,' Kirsty explained. 'Was that all right?'

I felt secretly relieved. 'Did you find anything?' she asked, undoing the girths on Lady's saddle.

'Yes, but . . . well, ask your brother,' I told her, and turned away from her interested eyes.

Later the headmistress of St Agatha's school telephoned. She sounded very grim, said she was considering Miss Allayne's report on the afternoon's incident and that she would be discussing the whole thing with the school governors. It was very likely that they would recommend taking the pupils away from Hillcroft.

In the circumstances I was feeling very glum and the knowledge that somehow the real culprit seemed to be getting away scotfree didn't help a bit. That evening, when everyone else had gone home, I sat in the tack room and tried to think of ways of attracting other schools to come in the place of St Agatha's. While I was doing this I heard a car turning into the yard. Sighing at the interruption, I went to look. The car was a somewhat battered Jaguar with Alan at the wheel.

8

He got out of the car and walked over to me. He was wearing a dark grey, three piece suit which made him look different, suave and sophisticated, as well as extremely good looking. It hadn't really registered with me before that he was a very attractive man and on the whole my mind was not particularly receptive to the fact at that present time. Perversely, for I suppose because of him I was saved further worry about bolting horses and so on, I blamed him for my troubles.

'Your precious Diane has most likely lost me the custom of St Agatha's,' I snapped at him before he could even open his mouth. 'But if you think that set back will make me sell the stables to you or anyone else, you're mistaken. We can manage perfectly well without the custom of a couple of dozen nasty little rich girls.'

His eyes widened at this unprovoked attack, and then narrowed. He seemed about to make some equally cutting return but instead said quite mildly, 'That's too bad about the school. But perhaps something can be done about it.'

'Such as what?'

'I don't know. I'll think about it.'

He followed me into the tack room and glanced round appreciatively. 'There's certainly a difference in here. You've worked hard, Lindsay. I've never seen the yard looking so smart.'

The unexpectedness of this praise threw me and made me feel as uncomfortable as I was sure he intended, for when he looked back at me there was amusement in his eyes. He said, 'I thought I'd better keep you posted. How about a cup of coffee?'

'All right.' I switched on the electric kettle and called over my shoulder: 'Diane wasn't here when I got back.'

'I know,' he replied.

I poured boiling water over the instant coffee and Alan picked up the two mugs and carried them across the tack room to where there were a few old armchairs and settees that had apparently been donated by various customers over the years, presumably to save themselves a trip to the junk yard. I sat rather carefully, mindful of recalcitrant springs, on one chair and he sat facing me.

'You shouldn't sit there in that suit,' I warned him, 'You'll get covered in cats' hairs.' He shrugged and sat down anyway. He took a sip of coffee and asked if I minded if he smoked.

'Of course not. Anyone can smoke as long as it's in here.'

'I'm a farmer. I'm not fool enough to smoke anywhere else in a stable.'

'Sorry.'

I relaxed back into the contours of the old armchair. It was strange to think that he and I were sitting here and not actually throwing the coffee at each other. I glanced surreptitiously at him but he was leaning back looking up into the dim corner of the tack room, where a pair of beautiful swallows had nested. He blew a ring of smoke into the air and his face in repose was quiet and contemplative. I found myself thinking, astonishingly, that he could be an extremely restful person to be with. He was so self-contained and full of self-assurance. He looked at me suddenly, getting at once to the point of the visit.

'I have something of an apology to make,' he said. 'You weren't entirely wrong when you thought Matthew Lawson might have something to do with all this.'

I sat bolt upright, my eyes wide. 'You mean, he *did* cause all those things to happen?'

'Indirectly.' Alan crossed one leg over the other and frowned. 'Apparently he met Diane and told her he would give her the job of managing the riding school, as his daughter didn't know too much about it, if you sold to him. He said you were being stubborn and hinted that it might help if you could be persuaded that running a riding school was too much trouble.'

'God!' I cried, sickened. 'That's dreadful. I suppose nothing can be proved.'

'Lord, no. Diane admitted to me that she slipped the lock on Lady's box — I owe you another apology, too, for calling you careless — and egged on young Colin to frighten the horses, though I don't reckon she intended any serious accident to happen. She got the idea because of the genuine accident that happened when Julia was here.' He looked sharply at me. 'I presume you wouldn't have her back.'

'Given the same circumstances, would you?' I demanded, and the tension eased as he gave a brief, rueful grin.

'No. I think you've been fantastically forebearing as it is.'

'Well! Of all the . . . The way you spoke I expected you to be on her side. You seemed to want me to forget the whole thing.'

'No! No, that wasn't it.' He straightened up, leaning forward, the mug cupped in his hands between his knees, the position somehow lending force to his words. 'But if you'd gone charging off in a tearing rage at her, in the end *you* would have suffered. You don't know this village, Lindsay. It's pretty cut off and horribly insular because of it. You're a newcomer, still probably regarded with suspicion by some. You've done well with the stables and increased your custom but that's because you're providing a very good service. But the Fairburns have lived here for generations. If you had an open row with Diane and chucked her out, most people would think you were to blame.'

'I . . . see.' I hadn't expected this, the serious intensity of his voice, this concern for my welfare. It was, to say the least, confusing and overwhelming. I hardly dared look at him for fear he should read how I felt about it, so I muttered at my feet: 'What should I do then?'

'Basically, nothing. I guessed you wouldn't want Diane back and frankly I don't think she would come. Just let well alone and it'll die down. She promised me she wouldn't tell any lies about why she left and she certainly won't tell the truth. Can *you* forget it?'

'I can try,' I said. 'I suppose I'll have to start looking for someone else.'

'I thought of that. I hope you don't think I'm interfering but the daughter of my dairyman left school last week and she hasn't found a job. She has her own pony and knows a fair bit about horses. I think she would jump at the chance to work here. She's not trained but she's young and strong and willing to learn. If you like I could send her along to see you. I think she would fit in well.'

'I . . . that's very good of you. I don't know why you should bother, but thank you.'

All this magnanimity was getting a

bit embarrassing for me though not apparently for him. From where I was sitting I could see his feet encased in shoes of highly polished black leather. He had relaxed again, his legs crossed, the stance very different from my own tense position. After what seemed like ages I got up the courage to say:

'I'm sorry about what I said that time, about you trying to get me to sell . . . and about Kirsty, especially about Kirsty.' Then I waited for him to gloat — I certainly would have felt better if he had, but he said nothing until I looked up, then he said:

'You thought I was being over-protective towards her.'

'I didn't realize how ill she had been. You see I'd . . . I'd had my fill of being over-protected myself. It's difficult to break away but I had managed it and I couldn't stand to see anyone else in that position.'

'Is that what you're doing here, breaking away?'

'Something like that.'

At that point I could see things getting a little too personal. Besides which, whereas I could cope with an arrogant, pig headed and chauvinist Alan Wentworth, this civilized, pleasant and disturbingly attractive man was something else altogether. So I sat up, looked at my watch and said in a brisk voice:

'Well, I won't keep you any longer, Mr Wentworth. Tell this girl to come along any time and I'll see her. And thank you for dealing with the Fairburns for me. I'm sure it's saved me a lot of unpleasantness.'

He made no attempt to stand up but merely replied, in quite a soft voice: 'Kirsty was right, you know. No one ever does call me 'Mr Wentworth'.'

For some reason it was the most embarrassing thing in the world for me to call him 'Alan' to his face, though I had been doing so in my mind for ages. I wondered what the heck was the matter with me. I was behaving like a Victorian Miss, blustering and blushing at the idea of calling a man by his Christian name. So embarrassed was I that I idiotically blurted out:

'All right . . . Alan. I'm Lindsay.'

He grinned. 'I know.'

I blushed even more and turned quickly to head for the sink where I could hide my embarrassment by washing out my coffee mug with unnecessary vigour. He came up behind me and put his mug on the draining board. I was so aware of his closeness that my hands shook. God, this was dreadful! I really was behaving like an idiot. Me. Lindsay Henderson. It would have been laughable if it hadn't been so bloody dreadful.

From behind me, though thankfully not too close, he said: 'I presume the horses are all settled for the night. Would you care to have dinner with me? I know a very good place about eight miles away.'

Astonished, I turned and stared at him, a dripping mug in both hands. He looked perfectly serious. 'But I thought you were probably going out with Diane!'

One eyebrow rose very slightly and his mouth tightened. 'I can't imagine why you should think any such thing,' he said, sounding annoyed. This was hardly surprising; I should have realized after the way he had talked about Diane earlier that despite her desire for intimacy between them there was none.

'I'm sorry. I didn't mean . . . '

'It doesn't matter. Actually I was merely going to have a drink with some friends. I can easily let them know I won't be there.'

I wanted to go — suddenly I knew that if there was one thing I really wanted at that moment, more than any other, it was to spend the whole evening with him. Yet I made excuses and had to admit it was because I was scared.

'I'm hardly dressed for it.'

'You can get changed.'

'It would take me ages. I need a shower and my hair should be washed.'

He had dug his hands deep into the

pockets of his trousers and stood a little way from me, feet slightly apart. There was no smile now but something else in his eyes, something I couldn't fathom. He said, very evenly, 'My dear girl, I — probably in common with ninety per cent of other men — would quite willingly wait quite a long time for a girl looking the way I know you can look. So don't make excuses of that sort. If you don't want to come out with me, just say so. I really won't be mortally offended.'

It was a strange time to be thinking of Martin, but at that moment I did think of him, and I knew that what I had felt for Martin, that adoration and admiration and passion, was nothing to the feelings I was now illogically and ridiculously feeling for this man. The urge to touch him — just to reach out and touch his hand or his arm — was so overwhelming that I clamped my hands together behind my back. And because my feelings were illogical and — let's face it — entirely unwanted, I behaved illogically, too.

'Thanks for asking me, Alan, but I'm really too tired to bother.'

Something flickered at the back of his eyes and he looked at me in a way that was unreadable. Then he shrugged.

'Okay. Another time perhaps.'

Would there be another time? I doubted it. He wasn't the sort of man to come back for another rebuff. I watched him go out of the door and turned away, sick with disappointment yet sure in my own mind that I had done the right thing. Just because I had felt so *physical* towards the man — after all he was big and tough and attractive, enough to make any girl fancy him — didn't mean I had to go getting involved, particularly in view of the reasons I had bought Hillcroft. No. I had been right to refuse his invitation. The look in his eyes when he had talked about waiting for a girl who looked like me had been far too full of raw desire. I, who was used to the light flirtatious ways of Martin and other men of his sort, wasn't at all sure I could cope with an Alan Wentworth.

I heard the low, throaty roar of his car starting up and then, much closer to me, came another noise that sent me to the far corner of the room to investigate. The noise, which seemed to come from a pile of horse blankets stacked up there, was a sort of squeaking or mewing. I reached the corner and peered closely, just in time to see Tigger producing her first kitten.

To say I was horrified is an understatement. Looking back on the situation later I realized that I behaved like the typical 'townie' that Alan had once called me. I suppose in a way that's what I was. Birth of any sort meant hygiene and antiseptic conditions, hospitals or the reassuring presence of a vet, and the fact that Tigger was making all kinds of extremely odd noises frightened the life out of me. Without giving a single thought to what I was doing, I charged out of the tack room screeching 'Alan!'

at the top of my voice.

Fortunately he had turned his car right round in the yard instead of just backing it out through the gate, otherwise he might well have been out of earshot. Also fortunately he had the window wound down and looked round at my shout. He stared at me as I charged across the yard and out into the lane.

'What the hell's the matter?'

I stopped, one hand on the door, gasping for breath. He probably thought a fire had broken out or something. 'Can you . . . can you come? It's Tigger.'

'Tigger?'

'The cat. She's having kittens.'

He stared in astonishment at me and then, much to my chagrin, burst out laughing.

'What's so funny?'

'You. I thought something drastic had happened. So — she's having kittens. Cats have been doing that alone and without help for years. She'll be okay. Just look in on her now and then.'

'But suppose something goes wrong.'

'Nothing will.'

'It might.'

He stared at me, his expression faintly bemused, then he sighed exaggeratedly. 'All right. Move out of the way.' He drove back into the yard and I hung about nervously until he had switched off the engine and got out of the car. Then I took him into the tack room and showed him where Tigger was. She hadn't had any more kittens and was still making the same noises.

'She looks fine,' Alan said easily.

'But she's making such odd noises.'

'I daresay you would if . . . ' He stopped, evidently having decided the comparison wasn't quite fitting. He looked down at me, his eyes still amused.

'I suppose you think I'm behaving stupidly,' I muttered defensively. He grinned but said nothing. 'I can't help the way I was brought up!' I went on crossly.

'I don't suppose you can.'

'We just didn't have cats that had kittens.'

'An unusual species indeed,' he said dryly and I detected distinct laughter in his voice. I still wasn't very good at being laughed at and flared up.

'You know what I mean! Don't be so bloody clever!'

His eyebrows rose. 'Now, now. That's no way to talk to someone you've come charging after to beg their help. Do you want me to stay or shall I go to hell as you seem to be wishing?'

'I want you to stay,' I muttered ungraciously.

'Right.'

He took off his jacket and tossed it over the back of a chair. The waistcoat followed. Then he carefully removed the gold cuff links that were in the white cuffs of his shirt, put them in his jacket pocket and rolled his shirt sleeves up to above the elbow. I watched all this in wondering fascination and he said by way of explanation:

'I don't for one moment think there'll be any complications but I may as well be prepared.'

As I had actually been getting an unwanted return of my feelings of wanting to touch him, this being brought on by the sight of his powerful and deeply tanned forearms, I couldn't think what to say to this, but merely muttered, 'What would you do if there were complications?'

'Get on the phone to Jack,' he replied, then grinned. 'I was joking. Look, I've acted as midwife to several assorted cows and mares, not to mention a whole flock of sheep when I was eighteen and spent a spring on Dartmoor helping a shepherd. I don't think I'm likely to panic over one cat.'

'No, of course not.' I glanced towards Tigger who seemed about to produce another kitten. 'I'll . . . shall I make some more coffee?'

'No.' He took my arm firmly, his fingers easily encircling my wrist. 'You're a country girl now. Sit and watch.' He very firmly pulled me down on to the sofa beside him and through the rest of Tigger's very masterful performance, I was hardly aware that I was pressed close against him or that both my hands were clasping one of his. I realized later though that he must have been very much aware of it. The births, five of them, seemed remarkably easy but I watched in fascination until Tigger, seeming to know it was over, pulled her head up rather tiredly and began to lick the little damp bundles. I breathed a deep sigh of relief and — I admit — pleasure, and turned towards Alan.

I'm not sure what happened next but I do know that one minute I was sitting upright feeling very pleased with myself for having watched the births of five kittens and the next I was lying virtually full length on the sofa, half pinned beneath Alan's not inconsiderable weight, my mouth crushed fiercely beneath his.

Hundreds of thoughts managed to

flash through my mind, not the least being that this was the loveliest thing that had happened to me, and though I couldn't breathe at all well and there were a couple of springs sticking into various parts of my anatomy, I managed to get my arms round him and return the kiss with enthusiasm. When I did this his mouth hardened even more on mine so that I gasped. He moved back a little then and smiled into my eyes.

'Are you comfortable?' he asked in a voice that was not quite steady.

'Not really. I think I'm being stabbed by a few springs. But I don't mind.'

He grinned and moved then, the sofa giving an ominous twang! that made us both laugh. He stood up and pulled me to my feet and back into his arms. On the whole vertical it was much better, with me being able to concentrate entirely on the matter in hand. He kissed me slowly this time, almost consideringly, his hands were warm on my back, pressing me against his hard body. It was sensuous, glorious, totally adult, totally unlike anything I had previously experienced.

Surprisingly, for the fervour in me sensed and responded to the desire that was in him, it was he who pulled away. His eyes were smiling but there was a different look in them now, an awareness and a quite open desire that made me feel weak. He put his hands on my shoulders and gripped them so tightly that it hurt a little, and said, his voice thick and heavy: 'I think, my lovely, that it's time we drew a halt because I am very rapidly losing what little control I have left.'

'I don't mind,' I said promptly, which made him laugh, though a little shakily. He bent his head and lightly kissed both my cheeks.

'You say that now but you might do in the harsh light of tomorrow. This has happened a bit too suddenly for you, Lindsay.'

The words were peculiar. 'For me? Not for you?'

He smiled faintly. 'Not for me. Silly

girl. Can you really tell me you don't know the effect you have on a man when you wriggle round in those tight jeans or . . . '

'I don't wriggle!' I cried indignantly.

'As I was saying, or turn up at the pub looking like the answer to a man's dreams.'

'I don't know what you're talking about.'

Briefly he pulled me back against him and spoke into my neck, his breath warm on my skin. 'What I'm talking about is that I've wanted to be doing this with you from the first moment I set my eyes on you.'

'Oh, Alan, no! You hated me.'

'I thought you were a selfish, spoilt little cat and I wanted very much to give you a damn good hiding. I also felt a quite primitive urge to toss you over my shoulder and carry you off.'

'Oh!' I thought of our first meeting in the light of this confession, but found it extremely difficult to imagine. There was no fathoming the male mind, I decided, and had just put my arms round his neck to tell him so when we both heard the sound of another car drawing up in the yard outside.

'Damn!' Alan muttered. 'Expecting someone?'

'Not that I know of.' I moved out of his arms and walked over to the door, automatically smoothing my ruffled hair down as I did so. I looked out, my breath drawing in sharply as I eyed the sleek, dark maroon Rolls Corniche convertible that was just drawing up beside Alan's car. The gasp died away to nothing, but there seemed to be a roaring in my ears when the driver got out and looked across the yard at me.

'Martin!' I shouted. 'What are you doing here?'

His eyebrows rose in that familiar, quizzical gesture that I had always thought so attractive but which I now recognized as being completely contrived. Even through my shock at seeing him I found myself wondering if he practised it in front of the mirror. At the same time he had glanced down at my feet, clad in rubber boots and back up again and, on seeing my rather scruffy jeans and shirt, the eyebrows threatened to disappear into his neatly brushed hair.

'My dear girl,' he drawled. 'What in God's name have you done to yourself? Does one have to look like a tramp in order to live in these surroundings?' The drawling, cultured voice grated on my ears and nerves far more than I would have believed possible a few months ago. It was a relief that I felt that way. True I was dismayed to see him but at least I wasn't intimidated or scared. I went over to him.

'What are you doing here? How did you find me?'

'Did you really think your father would let you run off in that most extraordinary fashion without attempting to find you?'

'No,' I admitted. 'But I didn't think he'd be able to find me. How did he?'

'To someone as wealthy as your

father, darling, all things are possible. And though I gather you thought you had covered your tracks thoroughly, in fact you left many clues easily discovered by the enquiry agency he hired.'

My eyes widened as I took in the full purport of this. 'My God! Do you mean he got a private *detective* on to me?'

'Something of that sort. Rather sordid I agree, but there. Your Papa is very annoyed with you, darling, and so am I, for that matter. However . . . ' Here he took hold of my upper arms and bent to kiss me. Unbelievable as it might sound, I didn't see the kiss coming and had no time to avoid it. Afterwards though I frowned and moved back.

'What do you want?' I asked sullenly.

'Uncle Robert intended coming himself as soon as he discovered where you were. But a small problem arose in the Manchester factory and naturally that took precedence.'

'Naturally,' I agreed dryly.

'So he sent me to fetch you back.'

'F — fetch me back?'

'Of course.' Again he looked as though he was going to kiss me but this time I avoided it by moving round the side of Alan's car. 'You've had your moment of rebellion, Lindsay, and no doubt it was great fun, though frankly you have let your appearance go in quite a frightful way. However, I suppose that can soon be remedied.'

'I'm not going anywhere with you,' I said coldly. 'So just go away. I don't know if your rotten enquiry agency told you but I've bought Hillcroft riding school and I'm running it. This is my life now and I've done it all on my own. I certainly don't intend to throw it all down the drain and go back to what I was before.'

Martin smiled in a maddeningly condescending way. 'Yes, darling. Uncle Robert said you would probably spout some such nonsense. Good Lord, my love, how could Robert Henderson's daughter carry on like this?'

'I have done so quite easily, thank

you, for almost three months.'

'Ah, yes, but I understand you have kept your identity a secret from all these rural types round here. You'll find they treat you rather differently once they find out who you really are.'

'But they won't find out. They don't know.'

'They don't know *yet*,' he said meaningfully, and though he was smiling I noticed how hard his eyes were. I wondered how angry and put out he had been because I ran away from him. It had probably bent his pride though I was sure his heart remained whole. The way he said 'yet' made me angry.

'You mean you would tell people? How low can you get?'

'All I'm saying, sweetheart, is that it's time you went home and started putting a bit of thought to our wedding. If you keep being stubborn I shall simply hang around for a while and if anyone shows interest in what I'm doing here, I shall tell them.'

'You . . . ' I began to say, but simultaneously his attention was caught by some movement behind me and I remembered Alan. I jerked my head round towards the tack room.

Alan was standing in the doorway watching us, and I had no way of knowing how long he had been there or how much of the conversation he had overheard. He had put his waistcoat and jacket back on and looked calm and unruffled. But there was an expression in his eyes that I didn't like one bit.

My introduction was ragged and ungainly, *not* the sort of introduction usually made by a girl who had learned the correct manner of doing these things at an expensive finishing school. The two men nodded to one another in a non-committal fashion and then Alan walked to his car and got in, though not before giving Martin's Rolls a long look. He said very formally: 'I think you'll find Tigger all right now, Lindsay. Nice to meet you, Mr Henderson.

You're the first of Lindsay's family to put in an appearance. She's been something of a mystery.'

'Oh, Lindsay is no mystery,' Martin replied smoothly. 'If there's anything you want to know about her, just ask me. I know *everything* there is to know.'

Not surprisingly, after that, Alan gave me a swift, ice producing look before starting up his car with an unnecessarily loud roar. Martin and I watched him go and before Martin could ask any awkward questions I turned to him and said: 'I'm not going with you, Martin, so get that into your head.'

He smiled as he got into his car. 'I noticed an hotel in the village, the White Horse. A bit rough and ready but I daresay it'll do. I'll put up there for a few nights. Goodnight, darling.'

'I won't change my mind!' I yelled at him, but he merely laughed as he drove out of the yard.

9

Not surprisingly, I didn't get much sleep that night. Later in the evening Jack phoned to ask if I would like to go for a drink at the White Horse but I refused with a vehemence that surprised him. Although probably he was one of the few people I knew to whom I could explain about Martin, I was not up to explaining anything over the phone, so I gave a headache as a fairly lame excuse. Admittedly it was doubtful that Martin would ever deign to take his immaculate and elegant self into the public bar of the White Horse but I didn't want to take even the smallest risk of meeting him and giving him the opportunity to talk about my family background as he had threatened.

Besides, there *was* the chance of meeting Alan in the public bar and that I was not ready for. My feelings for him were altogether too raw and uncertain. I had thought, as I was being kissed by him, that it was the loveliest thing that had ever happened to me. Now I wasn't so sure about that. I was beginning to think that being in love with him was going to cause me nothing but trouble.

The next day happened to be one of those on which Kirsty came in the morning and when she arrived, earlier than usual, I was already up and about. She expressed surprise at the fact that I had already done the morning feeds and brought in several of the ponies from the fields, but she was an incurious girl and didn't ask the reason for my industry. She simply fetched another halter and we walked to the meadow together. It was I who commented on the fact that she was early.

'I was glad to get out of the house,' she admitted. 'Alan got up in a foul mood and was stalking about the house frowning and snapping at everyone and everything.' She thought a moment.

'Actually he wasn't much better last evening, now I come to think of it. I can't imagine what can have made him so bad-tempered.'

We slipped the halters over the heads of two of the ponies that were among the crowd at the gate, all waiting hopefully to be brought in for their morning feed, and began to walk back down the lane. I didn't enlighten Kirsty as to why Alan was in a bad mood, but her words depressed me. It sounded as though he had heard most of the conversation I had had with Martin and no doubt his thoughts towards me were less than kind. I tried to convince myself that if he was angry that meant he was jealous, and that you don't feel jealousy unless you care about some- one. My optimism, however, didn't survive many minutes. Alan would have realized I had not been truthful with him about myself; he didn't know much about me but it was likely that at some time he would meet Martin again and learn the lot. I couldn't imagine Martin staying long at the White Horse — none of the bedrooms had private bathrooms and the cooking tended towards the heavier types of Olde English Fare, hardly the sort of cuisine to which Martin was accustomed. But he was unpredictable and might be prepared to ignore his creature comforts in order to punish me for hurting his pride.

After we had brought in all the ponies, we sat outside in the early morning sun drinking coffee and I told Kirsty that Diane wouldn't be coming back. She expressed surprise but not curiosity, seeming to accept that Diane was the sort of girl likely to up and leave, so I didn't attempt to explain further. We were discussing how the work load could be shared between us and Kirsty said she would work all day for a week or two, when a girl riding a bicycle came into the yard. She propped the bike up by the gate and walked over to us.

'It's Sarah Hayter,' Kirsty said. 'I wonder what she wants. Hello, Sarah.'

The girl looked about sixteen. She was tall and quite heavily built with a ruddy, smiling face and a matter-of-fact air that was unusual in one so young. She nodded 'Hello' to Kirsty but addressed me.

'Mr Wentworth sent me along, Miss. Said you might be looking for someone to work here.'

'Why, yes.' Surprised, I got up from the mounting block and dusted the seat of my jeans. I was surprised because after yesterday I hadn't thought Alan would want to do anything to help me. 'I gather you know quite a bit about horses.'

'I know a fair bit,' she agreed. 'I know how to muck out and clean tack, and Mr Wentworth said they'd be the main jobs.'

I laughed. 'We all help with those sort of things. But I certainly need someone to work here full-time to help in all ways. Come into the tack room, Sarah, and we'll talk about it.'

Actually, despite a semblance of an

interview, I knew almost at once that I would employ Sarah. She was exactly the sort of decent, hard working and sensible girl I needed, and Alan's recommendation was the final sway. He would not have mentioned her unless she had potential. I asked when she could start and she said at once, so that was one problem off my shoulders.

'It was a good idea of Alan's, thinking of Sarah,' Kirsty said.

'Yes. I'm sure we can work things well enough now, Kirsty. I may have to reorganize the timetable a bit during the week but with Jenny here weekends, those two days should be all right. You'll be able to continue having the weekend off.'

In the middle of the afternoon, after I had just finished taking a lesson, Sarah came out of one of the stables and called out: 'That Miss Thingummy, her with the French name, from St Agatha's, phoned. Said, could you ring her back? It's important. I wrote the number down.'

'Thanks Sarah.' I went reluctantly to the phone. Miss Deloitte would no doubt be confirming that she would be removing her pupils from Hillcroft. I dialled the number written on the pad in Sarah's large handwriting and gave my name to the secretary who answered. In a few seconds Miss Deloitte's cool, well bred tones could be heard.

'Ah, Miss Henderson,' she greeted me, sounding reasonably friendly. 'I thought I should let you know at once that we have decided not to remove our girls from your riding school.'

'Not? Oh!' I gulped with relief and went on: 'That's wonderful, Miss Deloitte. I'm so pleased.' Even to myself my voice sounded husky and emotional. I think that this was the very moment I began to realize in its entirety how much making a success of Hillcroft meant to me.

There sounded like a smile in the headmistress's voice as she continued: 'We are, of course, very pleased ourselves, for Miss Ursula has always given such good reports of your establishment and I know the girls are happy there. It was quite a relief when Mr Wentworth explained the situation.'

'Mr Wentworth?' I stared at the receiver as though it had suddenly become something alien to me, speaking words that didn't make sense. Breathing deeply, I pressed it to my ear again. 'Did you say Mr Wentworth explained?' I asked carefully.

'Why, yes. He came in during this morning and told me exactly what had happened. A very unfortunate affair which he assured me is unlikely to happen again. I realize that of course you cannot be blamed when a young hooligan starts playing about on his motor scooter — there is no way that you can be charged with carelessness.'

'Thank you,' I murmured, weakly. 'Yes, thank you.'

After she had hung up I continued to stand by the phone, receiver in hand, staring blankly ahead of me, until

Kirsty came in. She stared at me and said, 'What's the matter with you? You look very peculiar.'

'I feel it.' I replaced the receiver with exaggerated care and took another long, deep breath. 'That was Miss Deloitte. St Agatha's girls are to continue coming here.'

'Great. What changed their minds?'

'It seems Al . . . your brother went and saw Miss Deloitte and explained that the accident wasn't our fault. He seems to have persuaded her.'

'He would. Alan has a terrific line in persuasion when he want to,' Kirsty grinned. 'Fancy him doing that!'

'Yes. Why . . . ' I hesitated uncertainly. 'Why do you think he did? Because you work here?'

'Shouldn't think so.' Kirsty shrugged, seemingly unaware of how important this was to me. She went out, casually calling back: 'Maybe he was just in an altruistic mood. But I reckon he's got a soft spot for you.'

I waited in the cool dimness of the

tack room until I felt calmer and certain the hot flood that had heated my cheeks had subsided, then I got up and walked casually to where Kirsty was sweeping up the concrete walk that ran round the yard in front of the stalls. I strove to keep my voice casual.

'Where do you think your brother would be now?'

Kirsty grinned far too knowingly for my peace of mind and carried on brushing. 'Dunno. He might be helping Sarah's dad in the milking parlour or . . . no, I think they're starting to harvest the West meadow today. He'll be there.'

I nodded. 'I think I ought . . . I mean, I should thank him. It was very good of him, sending Sarah, and then going to St Agatha's. You and Sarah can manage the four o'clock lesson, can't you? It'll be good experience for Sarah?'

She nodded and went back to her sweeping, a small, secret smile on her mouth. I got the secondhand bicycle I had bought from a woman in the village out of the barn and set off peddling towards the West meadow. This was one of the fields farthest from the Wentworth farm; it was large and sprawled across a hillside, the wheat following the undulating curves of the hill, swaying in the wind like the waves at sea. I felt curiously light-headed as I cycled up the rutted lane that led to it, past other fields that had already been harvested. The only sounds were country sounds: some late lambs bleating in the distance, larks shrilling high in the blue sky; a blackbird in the boughs of a beech tree yelling at the top of its voice. Then I heard the combine harvester and in a moment the vast red monster came into view, moving up the far side of the field while a tractor headed towards me towing a trailer load of corn. I propped the bike by the open gate and stood back as the tractor came through, heading for the farm with its load. The combine continued on its noisy, dusty way, finishing that side of the field then turning and trundling back down the slope towards where I stood, the corn being stored inside it prior to being pumped into the empty trailer when it returned.

I waited. It was hot, certainly one of the hottest days we had had that summer, and the tension in my muscles didn't help. I could feel the sweat running in a very unladylike fashion down my spine and I took out a tissue and wiped my damp forehead. The combine came on and now I could see that Alan was at the wheel. I wondered what I would do if he chose to ignore me. I could hardly leap out in front of the great monster with its massive turning blades that sliced so easily through the wheat stalks. But almost at the bottom of the field, where he would have to do a reversing manoeuvre to turn the corner, the combine ground to a halt. A few seemingly never ending seconds went by and Alan did not get down. I realized that, having come this far, I must make the initial move.

He was, of course, deliberately

putting me at a disadvantage as it's not at all easy to talk to someone who is in the region of ten feet above you. I looked up at him, my eyes narrowed against the sun. He was stripped to the waist and looked hot and dusty; his hair was wet and his sun tanned body shone with a bright glow of perspiration. To me, at that moment, he looked far, far more desirable and sexy even than he did in the conventional suit he had been wearing the previous evening. In fact I was surprised and just a little shocked at the primitive feelings I had towards him then. They even momentarily drove away my nervousness and I forgot that we were not friends.

'I'm sorry to disturb you,' I shouted up. 'But I had to speak to you.'

'There's nothing you can have to say to me that's important,' he said gratingly and unpleasantly. 'Look, the forecast is for thunder during the next twenty-four hours and I have to get this field finished. So whatever you have to say, make it short.'

If he had kicked me in the face I couldn't have felt it more keenly. He spoke to me as though I were a nuisance, a pest like a gnat or a fly that needs to be swatted out of the way. It made me incoherent and robbed me of my earlier determination.

'I only wanted to say, thank you for Sarah. She came this morning. She'll be very good, I think. And Miss Deloitte phoned, she said you'd been to see her.' Suddenly I had the horridest feeling that I might cry, there in that lovely field of beautiful ripe corn with the scarlet poppies nodding their heads in the summer breeze, with the sun hot on my back and the sky an unbroken blue, with the man I loved staring at me with what I could only think was contempt. I would rather he had hated me than that.

He said, in the same coldly aloof voice: 'I sent Sarah because I said I would and I don't break my word. Besides, she's a good kid and needs a job. As for the St Agatha's thing, that was merely a matter of justice. Don't take any of it personally.'

There was nothing I could say. Perhaps once, a long, long time ago, Lindsay Henderson, that other Lindsay Henderson, the spoilt brat of a rich man, as he would so succinctly have put it, would have found something magnificently cutting to say to this man who was looking at her with such icy indifference. But this new Lindsay was crushed by that indifference, her buoyancy and happiness driven away by a man's few contemptuous words.

But he wasn't finished even yet. He went on: 'Now, would you mind getting out of the way? I have work to do, a business to run, and unlike some people, I'm not playing at it.'

I turned and walked back to where I had left my bike and at least I held up my head and did not cry. I knew what he meant. He had heard what Martin said to me last night. It seemed more than a little unfair that he should choose to believe Martin without giving me a chance to explain, but I supposed he wasn't entirely to blame. It really only confirmed his first opinion of me.

That evening was my lowest since I arrived at Hillcroft. I sat in miserable isolation, full of self pity, staring at the flickering television screen but aware of nothing other than my own depressed thoughts. I came near to wishing I had never seen Hillcroft riding school. It would have been better if my first encounter with Alan *had* put me off and sent me straight back home. Better never to have felt the satisfaction and joy of a job well done, such as I had felt when the cleaning up of the yard was completed, with the stable doors all painted a bright, sparkling blue; the muddy ground covered by a thick layer of hard pressed gravel; petunias, lobelias and allysum blazing brightly in pots round the yard. Better never to have had the girls tell me how much they enjoyed doing the graded training scheme and learning properly; better most of all never to have proved my own worth as an individual to myself.

I didn't believe it of course. Perhaps even that evening, when I brooded and cursed myself for being a weak fool, I didn't really believe it. Anything important has to be paid for and the cost is generally higher than mere pounds, and that was a very big lesson that I had never thought to learn.

One thing my previous life had taught me was how to hide my feelings. I might be miserable as hell because I loved a man who obviously had a very low opinion of me, but I was hanged if I was going to show it. That weekend, very much our busiest time, meant 'business as usual' for me. On Monday morning however I walked into the tack room to find Kirsty and Sarah talking in low, serious tones. I didn't catch what they said but it was obvious from the way they sprang apart and began trying to look busy, that I had been the subject under discussion. I pretended not to notice; after all, employees *are* entitled to talk about their boss, though

I did wonder what particular grievance they had to discuss in such a surreptitious way.

We got on with the usual chores and if Sarah looked at me in an openly curious way once or twice, and Kirsty in an almost troubled manner, I didn't really notice anything amiss until we were having the inevitable morning coffee. While we were drinking this I mentioned that I had pulled off a deal concerning hay with one of the local farmers and that this, along with the returning custom of St Agatha's, would make us much more solvent. Sarah, listening with the wide eyed, ingenuous stare that was the sole reminder that she was only sixteen, said:

'I don't see why it matters, Lindsay. I mean, why worry about a few pounds when all you have to do is . . . '

'Shut up, Sarah!' Kirsty snapped, the reprimand and the tone of voice she used so unusual that I stared at her in astonishment. She went on, in the same way: 'Go and get Rusty in. He's wanted for the eleven o'clock ride.'

Sarah went, not sulkily but hurriedly and guiltily. I leaned back in my chair and watched Kirsty with narrowed eyes. She was staring pointedly at the floor, avoiding my eyes.

'What was all *that* about?' I asked quietly.

Kirsty shrugged and stood up. 'Don't know,' she muttered, and then: 'I must start getting the water buckets scrubbed.'

I called her name sharply as she reached the door, and got up to face her as she came reluctantly back into the room. 'Come on, tell me. It's not like you to get shirty like that. What was Sarah going to say?'

'How should I know?'

'I think you do know. You've both been very peculiar this morning, looking at me as though I were different in some way. What's going on here?' When she still said nothing, I added: 'I thought we were supposed to be friends.'

'We are, but . . . ' Uncertainly, she picked up her mug of half drunk coffee and sipped it. 'It's only what people are saying. There's a man staying at the White Horse, a man who owns a fantastic Rolls Royce.'

I had, of course, guessed by then. 'My cousin Martin,' I said grimly, and she looked up, startled.

'Oh! Your . . . It's true then.'

'What's true? That he's my cousin, yes. Whether whatever else he's been saying is true, I can't tell until I know.'

'I only know what Sarah was telling me this morning, what her dad heard at the pub last night.'

'And what Alan said,' I wondered out loud, but she frowned and shook her head.

'Oh, no. Alan hasn't said anything. He never listens to gossip. Anyway, why should he say anything?'

'Never mind. Just tell me what Sarah's father said.'

She took a deep breath and met my eyes squarely though unhappily. 'Well, your cousin told him you only came here and bought the stables for a laugh, because you were bored and wanted to prove you could do something on your own, but that you don't intend staying and making a real go of it. He said there's no need for you to work at all because your father is a millionaire and that you're fabulously wealthy yourself. And he said that now you've got this taste for independence out of your system, you'll be getting rid of the stables and going home to marry him, which is what you were going to do before you came down here.'

It was far worse than I had imagined. Somehow I hadn't thought Martin would be quite so ruthless. Kirsty went on staring at me and I realized that she was waiting for a denial.

'What Martin said is true, but it's a distorted truth,' I said at last. 'It's true that my father is wealthy, and I have money, but most of it's so tied up in trust funds that I can't touch any. What money I did have has gone on buying the stables, and having all the improvements done — you know how much that cost. I did come here because I wanted to be independent, and maybe it was to prove something, but to myself, not to anyone else. I was being suffocated by my father, Kirsty.'

'That's why you tried to make me more independent of Alan.'

'Yes, but I see now that that was very different. Alan's reasons were kindness and love and genuine caring for you. My father's were nothing more than pure possessiveness. He can't bear to let anything that is his go. That's why Martin is here, to get me back because Daddy sent him, to get me back even if it means resorting to dirty tricks like making people believe I'm a spoilt, bored rich girl who will toss the stables away like an abandoned toy when I've finished playing with them. And I'll tell you something else, Kirsty,' I leaned forward, my voice shaking with anger. 'If *you* ran away and Alan found out where you were, he would come after you and try himself to persuade you to come back, but not my father. Oh, no, because he has some wretched business deal on that's more important.'

I felt suddenly sick and tears sprang to my eyes that I brushed away crossly. 'It's so bloody. All I wanted was to be ordinary, to be accepted as a normal person. I hated being looked on as Robert Henderson's daughter. I thought people round here were beginning to accept me.'

'They are,' Kirsty put in, her voice strained.

'Are they?' I muttered bitterly. 'They're all bloody quick to listen to Martin. I'm sure young Sarah is only thinking the way everyone else will, that if a person has a wealthy background they can never be serious about anything.'

'People are only curious. They don't mean anything by it.'

'Don't they? I'm not so sure.'

Kirsty walked to the door, frowning. 'The rest isn't true then, that you're going to marry your cousin?'

'That especially isn't true.'

She nodded and went out, but in less than a moment had returned.

'I don't get you, Lindsay. If your cousin is staying at the White Horse saying all those things and making people believe him, why don't you stop him? Go and see him and tell him you don't want to marry him and that you're going to stay here.'

'I have told him. He didn't believe me.'

'Tell him again then. Tell him till he does believe you. I'm darn sure I wouldn't let anyone spread a lot of stories about me in that way.'

She looked so fierce that I had to grin. Nevertheless, after she had gone I reflected that what she said was true. It was a bit spineless to pretend that if I ignored Martin he would go away. I should go down to the White Horse and make him understand that he had to stop what he was doing.

The thunderstorm that Alan had

predicted looked liked being on its way and just before I reached the pub, as I cycled along the village street, it began to rain. By the time I had reached the White Horse, where Martin's car stood in great splendour in the car park, the storm burst round me with frightening intensity. There was no shelter for the bike so I left it to get wet, and gratefully went into the building. Although it was not midday yet, Martin was in the lounge bar alone and looking bored to tears. I surprised the boredom on his face but when he saw me he quickly replaced it by what was supposed to be surprised delight. However, that earlier look had definitely been there and I could tell that after only two days, ruralizing was getting Martin down.

'Lindsay, my love, how delightful to see you,' he drawled in his usual way. 'What will you have to drink? Gin?'

I took off my waterproof anorak and hung it up. 'I don't want anything, thanks.'

'Nonsense.'

The landlord appeared and Martin ordered another Glenfiddich for himself and also a gin and tonic. I said sharply: 'It's much too early for gin. If you must, I'll have a lager.'

'How eminently plebian of you,' Martin remarked, having given the order. His eyes in their usual way were glinting under heavily bored lids but I wouldn't have said there was any humour in them.

'Martin, I want you to leave here. You're not doing any good, just causing a lot of trouble.'

'For whom, sweetie?'

'You know for whom! Can't you get it into your head that I'm serious about the riding school?'

'I never knew you serious about anything, my love.'

I stared bleakly at him. Was that true? Had I really been so shallow that now I was serious about something he quite honestly couldn't believe it? I felt the frown crease my forehead as I struggled to think how I might convince him of my sincerity. Into the silence that followed, a phone rang somewhere and then Mrs Pearce, the landlady, came into the bar.

'It's for you, Mr Henderson.'

Martin got off the bar stool. 'Don't go away, darling. We'll continue this conversation in a few minutes.'

I sipped the lager and thought despairingly about banging one's head against brick walls. It was tempting to make a bolt for it but since I was here I had to try to make Martin understand. I was thinking about that still, when he came back.

'Uncle Robert would like a word, Lindsay. He was most interested to know you were here with me.'

'Oh, Martin, no! For heaven's sake!'

He shrugged. 'You may as well talk to him. He's contemplating coming down here to add his persuasion to mine. Did you really think he would let you escape that easily?'

The telephone conversation that followed would have been recognized at once by anyone who knew my father. He was impatient, condescending, humouring, and as I listened I thought of all the other times he had been like this, from the time I was a small girl and had wanted one of the gardener's mongrel puppies for a pet. Daddy listened to my pleadings but in the end presented me with a highly bred poodle. Even then I had known there was no point in arguing.

But rather a lot of water had flowed under the bridge since then.

'I've been talking to Martin,' he said in a gruff voice, his first words to me in three months and not even an enquiry as to my health and/or happiness. 'He says you are being stubborn.'

'Not stubborn, just determined,' I began, intending to explain that I considered Martin's methods under-hand and also to tell him what I thought about him employing a detective agency to find me. I had no chance to offer either opinion however for he continued as though I hadn't spoken.

'Listen here, Lindsay, stop acting like a fool. You've proved whatever nonsensical point you've been trying to prove. I suppose Martin wasn't romantic enough for you, or some such rubbish. Well, you won't find a better husband than him, so you just get packed up and come back right now. I'll send someone down to deal with that stables place you've got.'

'Daddy, will you listen? I'm not — '

'You've had some fun, I daresay, playing at running this riding school, but that's all it is — fun. I never expected a daughter of mine to behave in such a fashion.'

'I'm not playing!' I bellowed down the phone.

He began to shout back and, recognizing the signs, I raised my own voice. 'Listen, Daddy, tell Martin it's no good, because I'm not marrying him and I'm not giving up the stables. And don't bother to tear yourself away from your precious business deals and come down to see me because you won't persuade me either!'

'Don't be a fool, girl. I'll cut you off without a penny!'

'I don't give a damn!' I yelled back and slammed down the receiver with a force that sent a powerful jerk up my arm. Though I was shaken by the conversation, it had not upset me. We had had many a row of a similar nature and basically they meant very little to either of us. It is a fortunate fact that people who care little for each other cannot really hurt each other and if there had ever been any real affection between my father and myself it had disappeared long ago.

I turned from the phone and Martin was standing there listening. Curiously enough that hard glinting light had vanished from his eyes and I felt that something had got through at last.

'You heard all that?'

'I should think everyone did, the way he was shouting. Did you mean that, about not giving a damn if he cut you off?'

'Do you think he will?'

Martin shrugged his elegant shoulders. 'It's all frightfully melodramatic and Victorian, but knowing Uncle Robert he just might.'

I took a deep breath. It's no good anyone being very smart and clever and saying it's that easy to give up something you have come to accept as part of your life. I had always known that one day I would inherit this vast fortune and now I had to look at myself with perfect honesty. I had spent what you might call my own personal fortune, the money my mother left me, on the stables and all the improvements made to them. If I accepted being disinherited I would also have to accept that like most people in this world I would have to earn my own living for the rest of my life.

'Yes,' I said slowly. 'I think I am prepared to accept it.'

'It's a big price to pay, for freedom.'

'I happen to think freedom is worth it.'

10

Martin gave me a long, considering look, then nodded and took car keys from his jacket pocket. 'I'll drive you back to the stables,' he said.

'I've got my bike,' I said, bewildered.

'You can't cycle in this storm. Leave the bike here.'

'But what are you going to do?'

He turned and looked at me, an odd little smile on his face. 'Let's say, you've convinced me. I personally think any girl who prefers to run a riding school when she could be married to me, must be slightly mad, but we'll leave it at that.' He walked to the door and opened it, revealing that it was still raining hard, the rain being driven at an angle by the wind in an almost continuous sheet, and thunder rumbled overhead. Martin shuddered, eloquently revealing his distaste for these surroundings. 'It seems you fit into this rural environment, my love, so good luck to you.' He turned and grinned at me. 'Evidently your big, tough farmer type will make you a far better husband than I could.'

I felt my colour rise. 'What's that supposed to mean?' I asked in a strangled voice, and his grin changed to a laugh.

'I was talking to a vet called Jack. He had a lot to say.'

As he then charged out into the rain, I had no chance to ask more. I followed him, dashing out to where his Rolls was parked, getting soaked in the short run. But once in the almost forgotten luxury of the limousine, Martin gave me a towel and turned on the more than adequate heating. I rubbed the towel over my wet face and hair and soon felt warm again. By then I didn't like to ask what he had meant by that final remark so I decided to pretend I hadn't heard it.

Martin turned on the windscreen

wipers and slowly edged the car forward. I wanted to tell him he was being ridiculous driving in this weather particularly in view of the narrow lane he would have to go along, but if I persuaded him to wait a while it would mean me having to hang about the White Horse as well. Now that he had decided to leave me alone and go home, I didn't want to risk doing or saying anything to make him change his mind.

I don't think he had realized what he'd let himself and his precious car in for. Even the Rolls' magnificent suspension protested a little as we bumped over the ruts. Martin muttered to himself then said: 'For God's sake, isn't there another way?'

I shook my head. 'I tried to warn you,' I told him meekly. 'And now you've come this far, you'd better keep going. There's nowhere to turn round and you might get stuck.'

He swore colourfully and we proceeded with due care, the gleaming sides of the Rolls missing the hedgerow on either side by inches. The rain continued to lash down and occasionally lightning flickered dramatically to the north. I managed to ignore Martin's cursing by fantasizing about what would happen if we were to meet another vehicle — a tractor for instance. It wasn't very likely; only fools drove about in this weather.

In the lay-by up ahead on the right, a Land Rover was parked. Someone waiting for the storm to pass, I guessed. But as we neared it I saw that the vehicle was empty. At the same time I recognized the registration number.

'Hang on a minute,' I said sharply, and reached to press the button that rolled down the window on my side. Rain splashed in on to the leather upholstery and the gleaming wooden dashboard, and Martin's protests were mixed with the noise of the rain on the roof. The Land Rover was parked near a gate and I could see the heads of a couple of cows that were sheltering near the hedge.

'What the hell's the matter?' Martin asked irritably.

'I don't know — probably nothing. Hang on a minute.' Even as I zipped up my waterproof jacket and pulled up the hood I realized how this country life had got to me. I sensed that something was wrong and it was unthinkable to go on by and forget it.

At least my footwear — I was still wearing riding boots — was suitable. I jumped across the puddles to the Land Rover and peered inside, but it was indeed empty so I went to the gate and looked round the field. The two cows near me glanced over incuriously but the main herd, across the field where the river was, were all staring at something more interesting.

I saw it then — or him — Alan, anyway. Martin, behind me, gave a yell to the effect that if I didn't hurry he was going on. I was struggling with the chain that fastened the gate but in the end it was quicker to scramble over. I went as fast as possible down to the river and the cows and calves that were there moved aside at my approach.

Alan was knee deep in the water with both arms round a calf that had slipped down the muddy bank and was threatening to be washed away by the already very swollen river. The silly creature was struggling wildly while its mother stood nearby lowing mournfully. The calf was quite large and the more Alan tried to get a foothold in the mud, the more the thing struggled and kicked.

Alan saw me. Afterwards I thought how easily he accepted my presence and put it to use. I didn't have to ask if he needed help — which he obviously did — or what I should do. He shouted: 'There's a rope in the Land Rover. Hurry!' And hurry I did.

The job was easy for him then. I was reminded of the quick and efficient way he had once hauled my sports car from a ditch. But this time, instead of standing there like a stupid 'townie' I slid down the bank into the water and helped steady the calf while he got the rope round it. Then it took only seconds to get it up the bank, release it and watch it run in a playful 'look how clever I am' fashion to its loving mother. Alan and I glanced at each other.

'Thanks,' he said abruptly and turned to stride back to the gate, with me following at a run. When we had passed through the gate, which he unlocked and held open for me, he stood still a moment, staring at the Rolls, his face unreadable. All the time the rain streamed down on both of us. I could feel that it had seeped through my thin jacket and was running in trickles of discomfort down my legs and into my boots. I didn't care one bit.

Martin leaned across the passenger seat and shouted; 'I hope you don't think you're getting in here like that. You must be out of your mind!'

I grinned. 'Probably. I don't want to anyway. Thanks for the lift, Martin.'

He shook his head, completely lost for words. I could see that he really was bewildered by my behaviour. He leaned forward to close the window. 'If you ask me, you two deserve each other,' he yelled. 'You're both bloody mad!'

The car drove, or squelched, away leaving us standing side by side in the middle of the lane. I was struck by the absurdest desire to laugh but I bit down that desire in case it should lead to hysterics. Instead I turned to walk towards the stables, which seemed the only thing to do.

'What did he mean by that?' Alan asked.

'Haven't the faintest idea,' I threw back over my shoulder.

'Hardly the way a prospective husband should behave,' he said. I stopped walking then and looked back. The wind blew my hood back and whipped my hair across my face.

'I'm not going to marry Martin. I was going to once but that was before . . . ' I could hardly say 'before I met you'. 'That was before I came here. I said all along that I wasn't going to marry him, that I was honestly trying to make a proper living through the stables. I'm not 'playing' at it — it's important to me, and I'm not being put off by you or anyone else in this rotten village who seem to think it's a crime for someone to have a rich father and then to try to make a life of their own on their own.'

Suddenly some of the water on my face was not just rain but scalding tears that I wiped away under the pretence of pushing back my hair.

He hardly seemed to hear half of what I said. He came up to me and said: 'You're *not* going to marry him?'

'I just said I wasn't!' I yelled, 'but you chose not to believe me. You chose to believe the worst without giving me a chance to explain anything.'

'That was because I . . . '

'Because what?'

'Damn it, you know why!' he bellowed. 'Because I thought everything was right between us, because I was way up in the air after what had happened in the tack room, then that joker of a cousin of yours turned up. I heard all that was said between you . . . okay, I shouldn't have just believed it, I was wrong and I'm sorry, but at the time it seemed the only thing *to* believe.'

'That's no reason for being so awful to me,' I said. We were both yelling at the tops of our voices, partly because of the storm but partly I think because it was such a joy just to be able to yell our feelings. 'I came to see you and thank you and you were horrid and sarcastic and beastly!'

'I was jealous!' he yelled. 'Can't you understand that? I love you like hell and I was bloody jealous.'

'You've got a bloody funny way of showing it, that's all I can say!'

At which point he decided to show me in a rather more conventional manner. The kiss was extremely wet owing to the fact that both our faces were soaked by the rain, but his lips were warm and determined and I felt a glow of warmth that was pure relief and happiness go through me.

'I always knew you were a number one Male Chauvinist Pig,' I muttered a few minutes later.

'Why?'

'When you kissed me in the tack room you made no mention of loving me, you only talked about men's baser instincts. And then there was the way you behaved when we first met.'

'Which you fully deserved.'

'And no one but a male chauvinist would tell a girl he loved her in these conditions. I'm soaked and my feet are buried in mud.'

Alan kissed me again. 'Surely, my love, that's a fine sign that I'm not just after your body, delectable though it might be. No one, looking at you at the moment, could possibly see where the attraction lies.'

'Well, really! You're no oil painting yourself!' I protested. 'And if that's the way you feel about it . . . '

'Shut up, woman, you talk too much,' he muttered, thus proving himself completely beyond redemption. Oh, well, I reasoned, accepting this treatment without demur. I never did go all that much on Women's Lib anyway.

THE END

We do hope that you have enjoyed reading this large print book.

Did you know that all of our titles are available for purchase?

We publish a wide range of high quality large print books including:
Romances, Mysteries, Classics
General Fiction
Non Fiction and Westerns

Special interest titles available in large print are:
The Little Oxford Dictionary
Music Book, Song Book
Hymn Book, Service Book

Also available from us courtesy of Oxford University Press:
Young Readers' Dictionary
(large print edition)
Young Readers' Thesaurus
(large print edition)

For further information or a free brochure, please contact us at:
Ulverscroft Large Print Books Ltd.,
The Green, Bradgate Road, Anstey,
Leicester, LE7 7FU, England.
Tel: (00 44) **0116 236 4325**
Fax: (00 44) **0116 234 0205**

VOICES IN THE DARK

Mavis Thomas

Lucy Devereux survives a car accident, but loses her sight. She also discovers she has inherited her grandfather's fortune. Then, to her horror and amazement, a young man comes forward claiming to be her husband. Lucy has no memory of him at all, but Doctor Harvey Sheridan thinks this could be due to her head injuries. Powerless to resist, Lucy is taken to live with her professed husband's family and soon finds herself a virtual prisoner. Convinced they are conniving to get her money, she appeals for help to Doctor Sheridan . . .